If I Lie

If I Lie   Corrine Jackson

Simon Pulse

New York London Toronto Sydney New Delhi

SIMON PULSE

An imprint of Simon & Schuster Children's Publishing Division

1230 Avenue of the Americas, New York, NY 10020

First Simon Pulse paperback edition August 2013

Copyright © 2012 by Corrine Jackson

All rights reserved, including the right of reproduction in whole or in part in any form.

SIMON PULSE and colophon are registered trademarks of Simon & Schuster, Inc.

Also available in a Simon Pulse hardcover edition.

For information about special discounts for bulk purchases, please contact
Simon & Schuster Special Sales at 1-866-506-1949 or business@simonandschuster.com.

The Simon & Schuster Speakers Bureau can bring authors to your live event. For more
information or to book an event contact the Simon & Schuster Speakers Bureau
at 1-866-248-3049 or visit our website at www.simonspeakers.com.

Designed by Angela Goddard

The text of this book was set in Bembo.

Manufactured in the United States of America

2 4 6 8 10 9 7 5 3 1

The Library of Congress has cataloged the hardcover edition as follows:

Jackson, Corrine.

If I lie / Corrine Jackson.

p. cm.

Summary: Seventeen-year-old Sophie Quinn becomes an outcast in her
small military town when she chooses to keep a secret for her Marine
boyfriend who is missing in action in Afghanistan.

ISBN 978-1-4424-5413-2 (hc)

[1. Soldiers—Fiction. 2. Best friends—Fiction.
3. Friendship—Fiction. 4. Secrets—Fiction.] I. Title.

PZ7.J132416If 2012

[Fic]—dc23

2011041112

ISBN 978-1-4424-4000-5 (pbk)

ISBN 978-1-4424-4001-2 (eBook)

To my sister, Kym—
You are my way home when I am lost.
Love,
Me

Chapter One

"Carey Breen is MIA."

His tongue weighs each word to cause the most pain.

My father's news drops like a bomb, blasting the air from my lungs, and everything in me shrieks, *Not Carey*.

My dresser bites into my backbone. I deflate, clamping my fingers around the Nikon to hide how they tremble. I want to throw up, but my father blocks escape to the bathroom, his shoulders spanning the doorway. Late February morning sun slips through the window blinds and swaths his perma-sunburned face in blades of light and dark. Shadow camouflage.

My stomach twists and sweat slides down my sides. He doesn't care what this news does to me. How it destroys me. His chin's up. Wintergreen eyes narrowed under sparse blond eyebrows. Hairline retreating from the neat rows of lines crossing his forehead. I'm barely holding it together, and he doesn't bother to hide his disappointment at my reaction to his words.

His lips thin. "Quinn, did you hear me?"

Yes, sir. Carey is MIA. Sir.

Since the scandal six months ago—*that* scandal we don't speak of—my father says Carey's name with reverence. They are two Marines, two men who've fought for a freedom I no longer feel. Comrades betrayed by the women they left behind.

Sand and grit have rubbed between the pleasantries in Carey's e-mails since I stopped answering him weeks ago. *We're leaving Camp Leatherneck soon*—pleasedon'ttell—*we'll be patrolling roads, clearing IEDs, something big's coming*—imissyou—*you may not hear from me for a while*—Godidon'twanttodie—*you must be busy with school and all*—talktomeQuinn—*I hope to hear from you soon.*

Carey could be a hostage. He could be dead, his brown body abandoned and decaying in a foreign country. The town has watched the CNN reports on Operation Moshtarak for the last week, tracking Carey's battalion, the 1/6, as waves of Chinooks dropped troops into Marjah. Rockets, machine-gun fire, mortars, and IEDs met them. I've held my breath for days, trying to pick Carey out in the news footage. What if . . .

Not Carey.

His parents must be destroyed. They know by now, if my father knows. How did they react? The Marines would have sent at least one soldier to the Breens' house, and I imagine how Mr. Breen looked hearing the news. Evaluating. Slow and methodical, his eyes focused on the ceiling to hide his thoughts. When composed, he would catch his wife's worried gaze, and Mrs. Breen would KNOW. As if she waited—expected—the worst to happen. Her body would fold, welcoming sadness, drowning in it, and Mr. Breen would support her, catching her before she hit the ground. If she blamed me before, it will now be a thousand times worse. I can't even grieve for Carey—not where people can see me.

Carey has sewed my mouth shut.

Pleasedon'ttell.

Nice girls don't cheat on their hero boyfriends. Damn you, Carey.

"Quinn?" My father sounds impatient.

My rage blows away, leaving hopelessness in its place. "I heard you, sir."

"You're not to leave the house unless it's to go to school or to work. People are going to be in a lot of pain when they find out. I don't want your presence making them feel worse. You've done enough, you hear me?"

I nod. He's right. Nobody will want to see me. Today, I will not go to Grave Woods. I set the Nikon on the dresser behind me, among the neat pile of lenses and memory cards. My hands feel useless without my camera. Void.

My father assumes I'll obey. His uniform has starched his backbone so straight he walks tall even in faded jeans and a worn Marine THE FEW. THE PROUD. sweatshirt. Lieutenant Colonel Cole Quinn's orders—like the Ten Commandments—are disobeyed at your own peril.

His eyes narrow to two dashes and sweep my room. They land on the bed with its sheets and blanket tucked military-style, as he taught me. The dresser with its clean top. The desk with the books lined up by size and subject. Nothing out of place. No thing to criticize except me. I cannot remember the last time his eyes stayed on mine. After I was branded the "town slut," he looks through me.

Maybe if we both wish hard enough, I will become invisible, with watery veins and glass bones. My translucent heart will beat on, but my father will not notice.

He sees only my mother in the spaces around me.

He leaves my bedroom door wide open. Moments later, my father's study door shuts with a *snick*. In his sanctuary, the bookshelves lining one wall tell the history of war from *A* (American Revolution) to *Z* (the Zulu Civil War). There are biographies of generals, World War II memoirs, and academic tomes about US military strategy during Vietnam. My father studies war as a hobby like other men hunt Bambi or rebuild classic engines.

A mahogany desk faces the Wall of War, and there are no chairs in the room other than my father's. I wonder if he has done this on purpose.

Holed up in his office, my father will not reappear until chow time at 1800 hours. Alone, I lie on my bed, pull the plain sky-blue bedspread over my head, and cry inside my tent.

The phone rings from the hallway—Dad took my phone

out of my room six months ago—and I pull myself together to answer it. Barefoot, I pad across the wood floor and into the hallway to the small antique sewing table that my mother restored a million years ago. It has the phone she put there. It's the old rotary kind, where you slip your finger into the holes and spin the dial for each number. Mess up and you have to start the process all over again.

"Hello?"

No answer.

The door to my father's office cracks open—his way of letting me know that he is listening.

"Hello?"

A sigh that's really more of a grunt comes in response. I know the voice, but he rarely speaks to me.

"Hey, Nikki," I lie. I lean against the wall and wind the spiral phone cord around my finger as if I'm settling in to talk to my old friend. My father's footsteps recede as he falls back to his desk. I grip the phone tighter.

"Talk to me, Blake," I beg in a whisper. "I know it's you." We hadn't always liked each other, but we'd had Carey in common. Me, his girlfriend; and Blake Kelly, his best friend who was more like a brother. We'd always kept the peace because Carey demanded that kind of loyalty. Despite everything that happened, that shouldn't have changed.

No answer.

"You heard, didn't you? Are you with his parents?" It made

sense. The Breens have turned to Blake for comfort since Carey received his orders. I'm guessing he's calling to tell me about Carey so I'm not blindsided at school Monday.

"Do they blame me?" I don't want to know, but the question scrapes out of me. *Do you blame me?*

Click.

"It's not my fault," I whisper, but Blake's gone.

There are some things nice girls don't do in a town like Sweethaven, North Carolina. Six years ago, before my mother walked out on us with my father's brother, she told me, "First chance you get, girl, run like hell. And for the love of all that's holy, don't end up a soldier's wife." A smudge of bitterness clung to the smoke from her Virginia Slims Menthol. Her Avon's "Light My Fire" red lips pursed around the filter one last time before she crushed the stained cigarette butt into the glass ashtray she hid whenever my father came home on leave. Short black curls spiraled in defiant abandon when she shook her head. "I wish I'd never seen *An Officer and a Gentleman*. Damn Richard Gere and his dress whites."

At eleven, I had no idea what my mother meant, but I understood one thing: My mother wouldn't pretend to be a nice girl forever.

With her tanned skin and snow-white sundress, my mother reminded me of actresses in the old movies she liked to watch. I had told her so, and she had caressed my cheek, the warmth of her fingers lingering for hours after. I loved my mom best when my father was gone. When his battalion deployed their fighting would cease, and the temperature in our house increased by ten degrees.

The summer I turned eleven, though, she dumped me at my grandmother's, dropped a kiss on my forehead, and told me to "be a good girl." She waved good-bye from the passenger seat of Uncle Eddy's Buick. It wasn't until my father returned a month later that I realized she wasn't coming back. And I could only blame myself.

After all, I'd told him the one thing sure to tear our family apart. I'd told my father that Uncle Eddy had slept in my mother's bed.

Located just west of Camp Lejeune, Sweethaven had a good number of sons (and some daughters) who'd enlisted straight out of high school. Many families could claim a Devil Dog in every generation, and all could agree: Cheating spouses were the scum of the earth.

My father returned from Iraq, and I trailed him unnoticed through our house. Tight-lipped and dry-eyed, he studied his uniforms, marching in solitary formation in the empty closet. My mother had committed one last sacrilegious act before escaping. His once pristine blue dress uniforms sported gaping holes from her best sewing shears.

My father's hand shook when he touched a brass button clinging to a jacket lapel by a single thread. I understood then the golden rule my mother had broken. You didn't disrespect the uniform. Ever. Not in a family that could trace five generations of soldiers who had served their country. Not in a town that could claim its forefathers had thumbed their noses at the British during the American Revolution and had lost sons to each war since.

My mother's name was not mentioned in our house after that day. And I—lovingly named Sophie Topper Quinn after my mother and my father's half-brother, Captain Edward Topper—became Quinn at my father's insistence. Quinn, the girl who would be better than her mother.

My father's epic ability to freeze people out had begun with my mother. Not that she'd ever tried to come back or see us again, but he'd managed to erase her from everything except my memories. He stripped her belongings from our house, barring the few things I hid in the attic. Their wedding photos disappeared one day while I was at school, along with every other photo of her.

Later, I wondered if I really remembered her the way she looked, or if she had become a screwed-up Debra Winger/Elizabeth Taylor collage. Other times, I caught my father watching me with cold, dead eyes, and I prayed he was remembering her, that my resemblance to her made him think of her.

Because I didn't want to believe my father hated me that much.

Especially when all of Sweethaven thought I'd become her too: the town slut cheating on her Marine.

Chapter Two

I can't sit still, and I can't stand to watch the news like I do every day. Men are dying and Carey's missing, but the reporters go on and on about which country has won gold medals in the Winter Olympics.

After I finish crying, I do exactly what my father has forbidden me to do. I stuff my backpack with my camera equipment, slip on my hiking boots and winter coat, and throw my long black hair into a ponytail. I hit the front door at a run.

My father calls out, "Quinn?" as I pass his study, and I pretend not to hear him. "Quinn, where do you think you're going?"

He reaches the front yard as I'm backing my Jeep out of the driveway. In my rearview mirror, he looks even more pissed off when my tires skid in the melted snow before gripping the road. He has already ordered me to lock myself away. What else can he threaten me with? The brig?

I need to forget Carey. My house/prison disappears, but the desire to escape hangs in air with the frost puffing from my mouth. The heater takes forever to kick in, but when it does I am wrapped in a cocoon of warmth. I need to remember Carey.

Every thought I have wraps around Carey. Just like it has since I first fell for him.

Fifteen, mouth girded in a dental chastity belt, a black nest of hair even a rat wouldn't sleep in, and gawky as hell—that's how I looked the first time Carey Breen kissed me. Me, Sophie Topper Quinn. A goody-two-shoes NOBODY of epic proportions. Forehead stamped: LONER, LOSER, LEFT BEHIND.

I'd loved Carey forever. Even before his body lengthened into muscles that would fly him right out of Sweethaven and on to grander things. At fifteen, any backwoods idiot could see he was meant for more than this tiny town. *A damned fool hero.* That's what some people called him when Carey stood up to that drunken bastard, Jim Winterburn, for beating the crap out of his little girl.

Everyone in the Sweethaven Café had seen Jim backhand Jamie, punishing her for her clumsiness when she tripped and fell into him. Jamie had grown faster than the other girls in my ninth-grade class, and she teetered around on her spindly limbs like she was walking around in her mom's glittery, four-inch high heels. Every day was Roulette Day with Jim Winterburn. That day, the wheel stopped, the ball dropped into the Preteen Clumsiness slot, and Jamie's cheek lit up from her father's hand.

People say Carey was lucky to have walked away from that fight. Jamie's dad had fifty pounds of muscle and a decade of pissed-off on a fifteen-year-old boy. Jim had fed on bitter hatred so long that the blood pulsing through his veins had hardened to petrified liquor. Hate for the government, hate for the war, hate for the town he'd returned home to, shy one arm and a chunk of his intestines.

"Jim never really came home from Desert Storm," I overheard my father once say to one of his Marine buddies. I'd bet Jamie and her red, white, and blue body would have begged to differ.

Jim struck Jamie, but it was like he flicked a match on embers that glowed inside Carey. He called Jim a "yellow-bellied coward," the worst insult you can toss at an ex-Marine, aside from calling him a traitor outright.

Twenty adults watched in shock as Jim tried to pound Carey into the diner's cheap linoleum floor. My dad and the sheriff were among the first to jump in to put a stop to things. Blood had turned Carey's brown hair black, and one of his eyes had already threatened to swell shut. He'd never raised a hand to defend himself, but a triumphant Carey laughed in Jim's face as the police hauled him away.

Years later, Carey confessed he'd done it on purpose, letting Jim swing away. The Sweethaven townsfolk might not step into the middle of a domestic-violence situation, but they couldn't ignore a public attack on him. That's the kind of guy he was. He couldn't stand seeing Jamie hurt, so he'd done what he had to. Nobody could take a hit like Carey.

Damned-fool hero Carey. SOMEBODY Carey.

So, a year later, when he caught me behind the gazebo at the town's Fourth of July picnic and kissed me crazy, I thought it must have been on a bet, and punched him in the stomach. For crushing the sweet new feelings I had for him.

Of course, my scrawny fist didn't have the impact I'd hoped. Carey just laughed and hugged me and whispered that he loved me and asked would I be his girl?

Would *I* be his girl? Stupid, lonely, ugly *me* be his girl?

He saw my disbelief like he saw everything else about me. To Carey, my guts had been sliced open and turned inside out so no secrets remained. His fingers trembled in mine, and he brushed his lips against my knotted fist. He knew my fear like it was his, as if the same monster lived and breathed in him.

"I won't ever let you down," he promised, his voice cracking a little.

And I believed him.

I don't want to be alone, but I don't really have anywhere to go.

Eventually, I end up at Bob's Creperie. Sitting at Bob's sounds better than driving and thinking in circles. At least the restaurant has coffee and a heater that doesn't quit.

Despite their name, crepes aren't on the menu at Bob's, but

every kind of pancake is. Banana pancakes, whole-grain pancakes, maple-bacon pancakes, whatever-you-want pancakes for the regulars like me.

Longing to go unnoticed, I slide into a booth toward the back, away from judgmental eyes. Denise Scarpelli, who sometimes used to play poker with my mom, comes over, unhurried now that the Saturday morning rush is over. Obviously she hasn't heard about Carey yet because she doesn't spit in my water before handing me the glass. Instead, she takes my order for pecan praline pancakes and walks away.

Nothing matches in Bob's. It's decorated with tag-sale tables and chairs of every style and size. The place reminds me of better times, when Carey, Blake, and I used to come here on weekends before Carey went off to basic. Blake and I haven't bothered to keep up the tradition since Carey left. Too much water under that bridge.

I can't think about how life will change if Carey never comes home.

I'm scooting untouched pancakes around my plate when the front door swings open and a bunch of girls from our school's cheer squad walk in. A few of them sport red, splotchy cheeks and look like they have been crying, including Angel and Nikki. They must know about Carey. Like me, they've come to Bob's for pancakes and comfort. When Angel spies me, she tenses with anger, and I know my father was right. Seeing me makes things worse for everyone. Six months of hating me and this news will only feed their rage.

I throw money on the table to cover my check and rise to leave. I feel their eyes on me, and shame heats my face.

I bargain. *If I can just make it to the door, I will never show my face here again. If I can leave without being humiliated today, I will take whatever my old friends dish out tomorrow. Just please, not today, when I feel bloody and raw.* I'm almost past the squad's table. *Please . . .*

A foot sneaks out and hooks my leg. I crash to the tiled floor, my knees and one elbow breaking my fall. Nobody laughs in the sudden silence. I gasp in pain.

"Watch where you're going, slut."

Nikki. Her eyes narrow. She hates me, but usually she's just a follower. Jamie starts most of the crap. Jamie, who has loved Carey ever since that day he saved her from her father. Today, with the news of Carey's disappearance still fresh, Nikki doesn't need Jamie to humiliate me.

Clamping a hand on their table, I pull myself to my feet. A tear leaks out and my knees throb like hell. Angel won't even look at me, her petite face turned away as if to deny I exist.

Anger has saved me every time they've hurt me these past few months, but I can't find it now. Maybe because I think I deserve this in some twisted way, though not for the reason they think. Embarrassment flickers through me, and I shrink under the weight of everyone's judgment.

I force myself to find a backbone, and lift my chin in defiance. Nikki flinches like I'm going to hit her when I lean forward. As if.

"Did that make you feel better about Carey, Nikki?" I ask in a quiet voice.

She crosses her arms and drops her gaze, in a small way acknowledging that Carey would have hated what she just did to me. He always rooted for the underdog, and they all treat me like a dog these days.

"Me neither," I whisper.

The silence is terrible. Angel finally grounds out, "Just leave, Q. Nobody wants you here."

From anyone else, those words would have hurt. Coming from Angel, they make my breath hitch in a sob before I stifle it.

I limp to the door, bruised in places they can't see. And I feel pathetic, because all I want is for one of them to be my friend again and tell me everything will be okay. Six months ago, they would have. I took it for granted.

You never know what you have until it's too late.

Ten months ago, Carey had come home for a brief leave. He had graduated a semester early so he could start BT sooner. For the three months he'd been gone, we'd only spoken through letters and a couple quick phone calls.

If he had seemed different that May, I ignored it. I was too relieved to have him with me again. If it seemed like he didn't have a lot of time for me during that leave, I ignored that, too, because I thought, like me, he might be struggling with the separation looming before us.

The last time Carey, Blake, and my friends were all together was on Carey's last day of leave. The Breens had thrown a party to celebrate his graduation from BT and his departure to Camp Geiger, where he'd make the transition from Marine recruit to combat-ready Marine. I hated the sound of "combat ready" and all that went with it, but Carey wanted to be a Marine more than anything. So I supported him, and arranged a surprise after-party. A party parents weren't invited to.

Angel and Nikki helped me plan everything and decorate Blake's house early in the day. They handled getting everyone there, and my job was to bring Carey. He thought I'd planned a quiet night at Blake's, just the three of us, so he was shocked when fifty of his friends erupted in cheers and hoots when he walked in the door.

Blake gave Carey one of those half-hugs guys give each other, smacking him on the back. But Blake avoided my eyes like he'd done for the past few months.

Carey, overwhelmed by our surprise, hooked one arm around Blake's neck and one around mine, yanking us into a close circle. Blake seemed to stiffen for a moment as he brushed up against my side before relaxing and returning Carey's grin.

"I love you guys," Carey said.

I shot Blake a small smile. "Would you believe he's not even drunk?"

"We can fix that." Blake pulled away and headed off to the kitchen where the keg lived.

Carey wrapped both arms around me, and I tucked my cheek against his chest.

His chin on my head, he said, "What's up with you and Blake? Did you fight?"

He never missed anything where I was concerned.

I shrugged. "You know Blake. He's always hot and cold with me. Really he only puts up with me when you're here."

A warm hand smoothed down my back. "You want me to talk to him?"

"Nah." I squeezed his waist. "I missed you. I hate that you're leaving tomorrow."

Something shifted in his expression. Something I couldn't read. Carey opened his mouth to speak, but Angel and Nikki interrupted.

Angel shoved us apart. "Give us a break, Barbie and Military Ken. You look serious, and that's definitely not allowed tonight. We're here to drink, party, and be a little reckless." She smacked a loud kiss on Carey's cheek. "Don't worry about your girl, Care. Nikki and I'll take care of her."

He grimaced. "That's what I'm afraid of."

Nikki slugged him in the gut. "Hey, we're cheerleaders. We excel at cheering people up. Though I'm not sure why Q would be sad about your sorry ass leaving."

He just laughed and mussed her hair.

Blake returned with red plastic cups of beer and passed them around.

Somehow I ended up on the couch with my legs thrown over Angel's lap.

She rolled her eyes. "Who invited Jamie? I swear, if she throws herself at Carey any harder, I'm going to kick her ass."

I followed Angel's gaze to the other side of the living room, where Jamie wrapped her arm around my boyfriend's waist. Carey tried to sidestep her, but Jamie followed, trailing a hand down his arm. Blake stood behind him, cracking up while he watched the whole scene. Carey shot me a pleading glance, and I grinned, blowing him a kiss. Blake's smile turned into a frown, and I stuck my tongue out at him, wondering what the hell his problem was.

"Carey can handle her," I said to Angel. "But I should probably go save him. Come with?"

I stood and helped her up, then we headed toward the boys. Jamie scowled when she saw us.

"Why do you put up with her?" Angel asked. "It's gross how she's always crawling over him."

"I'm not happy about it, but I trust Carey." I didn't add that I felt kind of sorry for Jamie. It had to be hard growing up with Jim Winterburn for a father.

Angel sighed heavily, and I bumped her with my hip. "What?"

She smiled. "Nothing. I'm just jealous of you guys."

I raised a brow. "You're jealous of how I've just spent three months alone and how it'll be August before I see Carey again?

Or maybe you're jealous of how he'll probably be in Afghanistan or Iraq while we finish out our senior year?"

I tried to keep my tone light, but Angel must have heard my unhappiness. She hugged me. "Well, when you put it that way, who doesn't want a Military Ken? Seriously—you know I'm here for you, right? And Nikki will be too."

With perfect timing as ever, Nikki let out a shriek of laughter. Gabriel Palucki had yanked her onto his lap and was tickling her to her obvious delight. Angel and I shook our heads. Where the boys were concerned, Cyclone Nikki left a devastating path.

"Okay. *I'll* be here for you," Angel amended, and we snickered.

Familiar hands clamped on my shoulders from behind and turned me so I was facing Carey and Jamie again. I looked over my shoulder into Blake's shadowed hazel eyes, and he pushed me forward.

"Do him a favor, and save the poor bastard. He's too polite to tell Jamie to go to hell."

"Yes, sir!" I mock-saluted him, and Blake scowled again. "You keep looking at me like that, Blake, and your face is going to get stuck that way."

Finally his expression lightened up and he laughed, against his will, if I had to guess. I headed for Carey, whose eyes lit up when I launched myself at him. He caught me in midair, holding me against his chest, and I looped my arms around his neck.

"Good-bye, Jamie," I said, without taking my eyes from my boyfriend's. "Things are going to get embarrassing if you stand there watching us kiss." My feeling sorry for her only went so far. She needed to keep her hands to herself. Out of the corner of my eye, I saw her slinking away, her cheeks flushed a brilliant red.

Carey planted a chaste kiss on my mouth, rather than the passionate one I'd wanted. He'd done that a lot that week. Maybe he saw my disappointment, because he kissed me a second time, lingering a little longer.

"What's the matter?" I asked, sensing something was off.

"Nothing." He squeezed me tighter when I continued to frown at him. "What could be wrong? I have the best friends in the world and I have you. Things are perfect."

We were pulled apart again by friends all wanting to spend time with Carey before he left. He had a way of making people feel special, and I couldn't blame them for wanting a piece of that.

But later, I wondered if I should have pushed Carey that night.

Our last perfect night together had somehow felt like the beginning of the end.

Chapter Three

On the way home from Bob's, I accidentally-on-purpose steer the Jeep down Carmichael, Sweethaven's main street. Breen's Auto Body sits in the middle of the block, and Blake's motorcycle is parked to the side of the ancient brick building. For the past two years he's worked at the garage after school and on weekends. Carey's parents have taken him in as a kind of surrogate son since Carey left.

On days like today, I envy him. I wish I could be with the Breens, grieving with them instead of driving around alone. I am so sick to death of myself. Of the loneliness that has cleaved itself to me like a disease. People can tell I'm in quarantine from a mile away, and they avert their eyes and hold their breath so they don't catch what I have.

My foot eases up on the gas when I see Blake bent under the open hood of a station wagon. On impulse, I pull into the garage's driveway. He hears the sputtering of my engine—he's worked on it many times in the past—and his head turns toward me. Our eyes meet, and I wish I could read his mind. I once thought I knew his moods better than anyone's, except for Carey's. But Blake has become a stranger.

He straightens and glances around, wiping his hands on the dirty rag tucked into his back pocket. I know he is checking to see if Mr. Breen is around to spot us together. Nobody but him seems to be working the Saturday evening shift. Blake hesitates a moment longer before walking over. He climbs into my passenger seat, easing my camera case onto his lap to make room.

Black hair. Muddy hazel eyes. Whipcord lean, muscled body. Masculine but not really handsome.

Blake is nothing like Carey. Negative to positive. I think their differences were the basis of their friendship. Each was what the other wanted to be.

"How are you?" he asks finally, staring at a splat of gray bird shit on my windshield.

"Seriously?" I say with a short laugh.

He sighs. "What do you want from me, Q?"

The truth, for a start. Maybe a lie to make me feel better.

"This isn't the best time for you to come around. I wouldn't even be here, except I offered to finish up for Mr. Breen."

It's hard to look at him, so I watch the shop's Stars and Stripes snap and snag around the flagpole. "I wondered if you'd heard anything about Carey. The last time he wrote me, he was headed to Marjah. Is that where he went MIA?"

Blake's surprise is palpable. He didn't know I still talked to Carey. "You know how it is. The military isn't telling the Breens much. His unit was on a scouting mission, hunting for IEDs. They got pinned down by snipers. The rest of his unit made it back, wounded but alive. Carey wasn't with them."

I imagine it like it's a spread in *National Geographic*. Carey in his dusty camo, focused on doing his duty and trying not to be a target. Wondering how he can save everyone. Marjah's one of the last Taliban strongholds in Afghanistan's Helmand province. Poppy fields keep the local opium suppliers in business and the insurgents funded. Taliban soldiers use women and children as human shields and take cover in civilian homes. Marines are dying, fighting an invisible enemy.

"God! Why the hell did he have to go there?"

A smile lifts one side of Blake's mouth. "Because he's a damned hero."

He hasn't smiled at me in months. Not since before Carey left. If only I could snap a portrait of him and frame it for the hours I spend alone. I think about Blake's mouth on mine and yearning spirals in my belly. Carey, I have loved for years, but Blake makes me ache. I don't feel safe with him. I feel alive in a way I never did with Carey. That should have been my first clue.

I pull my gaze from Blake's mouth and realize he is staring at my lips too. Maybe he is remembering. His eyes take on that tortured look he's worn for months. It's my fault. My silence put that expression there.

My jaw unclenches to tell him the truth that would set us both free: *We. Didn't. Cheat.*

Three little words. A breath and we could comfort each other. Hold each other.

But he says, "You can't be here, Q. It hurts the Breens to see you."

I recoil. "What about you, Blake? I wasn't the only one in those pictures." *Just the only recognizable one.* In the picture, Blake held me, our clothes more off than on, but his back faced the camera. Innocent, due to the bad angle the photo was shot from.

He hunches his shoulders like he is warding off a chill. My camera strap is wound around his hands, and I study the grease creased into the side of his nails. Funny. He hates having dirty hands.

"I'm sorry," Blake says to my windshield. "But I don't think it would help them if I told the truth. I don't want to hurt them any more than we already have."

He looks like a hero for supporting the Breens, both emotionally and at the shop, while I continue to take the blame alone. My knees and elbow throb as a reminder. I don't understand how I can simultaneously want to both hit him and touch him. Once upon a time, he was my best friend besides Carey. Back when I was still Carey's Quinn.

"Why did you call me? I know it was you."

You wanted to hear my voice. You missed me.

"I thought you should know about Carey. So you could steer clear of the Breens."

I close my eyes and inhale one, two shutter clicks. "Get out," I say calmly. He's reaching for the door handle when I say, "You're a coward. You know that, right?"

He stiffens and, for an instant, he reminds me of my father. Then he shakes me off with a violent twist of his arm. "Fuck you, Q. After what you did, you don't get to judge me."

The Jeep door slams behind him, and my camera bounces on the seat where he threw it. He stalks back to the garage, and I put the Jeep in gear. If Carey were here, he would have poked at Blake until he stopped acting like a prick. Then Carey would have scolded me for being such a bitch to Blake because the guy was doing the best he could, given the circumstances. If Carey were here, I would tell him to take his damned secret and shove it.

But he's not here. And I won't break another promise.

So I will pretend we were still together when he deployed, lying to our best friend and everyone who hates me for cheating on him. And I will forget that he broke up with me two days before those pictures of Blake and me were taken.

Because then I would have to remember how Carey had admitted that he loved a boy.

My father is in his garden when I get home.

The permafrost is melting, and he is itching to get his hands in the dirt. His gardening obsession started the year my mother left. Each winter, he kills hours mapping out the rows of fruits, vegetables, and herbs that he will plant. March arrives, and he fades from the house, consumed with preparing the soil for the seeds and bulbs he's cultivated from last year's harvest. He tends to the plot of land with the tenderness of a sweetheart caring for his lover.

Carey and I used to laugh at him. At the way he would force the land to grow at his command. This year, I'm not sure I can stand to watch my father dote on his plants.

He sees my Jeep pull into the driveway, but he ignores me, stomping through the dirt and snow. He pauses to test the fence he put in to keep the rabbits out, and his chest heaves with the exertion.

I try to remember what he was like before my mother left, but it's hard to call up a clear picture. After 9/11, I felt more of his absence than his presence in my life. And when he made it home, he spent his time preparing to go back.

My mother hated it. She said he used to be fun and paid more attention to us. She hated how the war changed him and how he was always gone. Enter Uncle Eddy, who was assigned a post on base. He had one huge thing going for him: He stayed behind.

I was supposed to be at Carey's.

In those days, I was one of the boys. We had plans to build a fort, and Carey had invited Blake, the new boy in town, to join us. At twelve, Carey and Blake should have been too cool to play with me, but I wasn't like other eleven-year-old girls. For one thing, I was a better shot with Blake's BB gun than the two of them put together. I could snag the head from one of Mrs. Murphy's tulips from the oak tree in Carey's yard. For another, I thought bows and ruffles were the devil's invention, and I dressed like a boy, except when my mother got her hands on me.

My birthday had come and gone. My father hadn't been able to make it to my party, but my mother said he'd called the night before while I slept and had told her to wish me a happy birthday. She said this every year except for the two he managed to make it home. But by then I'd figured out the truth: My father didn't care. My mother didn't have the heart to lie anymore, nor did I in my response.

My uncle Eddy had given me a digital camera. My mother argued the gift was too expensive for a child, but Uncle Eddy just laughed and ruffled my hair. Carey wanted me to take pictures of the finished fort, but I had forgotten my camera at home.

I rode my bike all the way back to get it.

When I arrived, I noticed my dirt-covered jeans and sneakers and knew my mother would kill me if I trailed mud through the house. I kicked off my shoes and brushed the worst of it off my jeans. In a hurry, I snuck into the house in my socks, tiptoeing around the two spots in the hall that squeaked.

If my mother hadn't sneezed as I passed my parents' room, I never would have peeked through the open doorway. My uncle lay in my parents' bed, his blond head on my father's pillow next to my mother's darker head. In his sleep, he shifted and threw an arm around her waist, curving against her back. A sheet covered them, but I could see they were naked beneath the crisp white cotton. A mysterious musky scent hung in the air.

A small sound of confusion escaped me.

My mother's mouth formed a small O as she sat up, exposing her breasts before she grabbed for the sheet.

"Sophie!"

I ran. I didn't stop until I reached Carey's house. By the time I arrived, I was crying so hard my words came out in waves of hiccups and gasps. Blake had already gone home, but Carey sat next to me on his front steps, his shoulder warm against mine as he waited for me to calm down.

And when the tears stopped, I told him what I saw. He held on to my hand, and we waited in silence for my mom to come find me.

Dinner is a sit-down affair at our house, and tonight won't be any different. Since my mother left, my father demands we eat at our dining room table at 1800 hours every night. We exchange maybe five sentences on a good night. Land mines pepper our conversation.

"How was school?" *How did you screw up today?*

"Good, sir." *It sucked.*

"You did your homework?" *At least you have good grades (i.e., are not a complete failure).*

"Yes, sir." *The better to escape Sweethaven.*

"Make sure you load the dishwasher. I have work to do in the study." *I'd rather work than spend five more minutes with you.*

"Yes, sir." *Please look at me.*

Then he goes to his office and I go to my room. We are housemates. At some point, my father stopped loving me. I have spent hours and days trying to figure out how to fix what's broken between us. I've spun a thousand fantasies that all end with him saying he loves me. Then the voice in my head overrides it all, shouting, "You're a freaking idiot! He doesn't give a shit about you!"

That Saturday night, our usual strained exchange is not what waits for me at dinner.

Some silences feel like sliding into your favorite slippers. Carey and I could sit for hours without talking. He'd lounged on one end of our couch with a video-game controller in his hand, and I'd stretched out on the other end with my nose in a book. Some part of us always touched, whether my feet rested on his thigh, or his elbow leaned on my knee. Comfortable, familiar quiet.

There are also punishing silences that howl through a room like a Category 5 hurricane. Whole towns are destroyed by my father's silences.

He doesn't ask me where I went when I left the house. Most likely he already knows, since it's easy to keep tabs on me in a town where everyone knows everyone. He passes me a plate of peas, instant rice, and steak, and I sit across from him at our round table. The entire force of his considerable concentration is focused on eating. I see his strategy—to ignore me—but knowing that doesn't make it any easier to withstand. He cuts his steak into small, equal pieces, but I am the one he slices.

Me:

Him:

The peas have rolled into the rice like green snow on white grass. I use my fork to separate them, and shovel a few into my mouth.

The muscles in his forearms shift. Fork to mouth. Chew. Cut. Fork to mouth. Finally he rises, rinses his plate, and leaves the room.

A direct hit, sir. I salute his back with a nonmilitary gesture.

And wonder how he's missed that I've been a vegetarian for more than a year.

Chapter Four

Sunday morning I drive fifteen minutes west to Fayetteville. The parking lot at the VA Medical Center is more than half full. The weekenders are arriving to visit their loved ones. I park farther out and ignore the shuttle, preferring to walk in.

Comprised of eight buildings, the hospital serves more than 157,000 veterans in twenty-one counties. Overwhelming to the uninitiated, the five-story redbrick buildings look more like a college campus than a hospital. In the main building, Darlene waves from the front desk as she directs a distraught fortyish woman to the second floor—ICU—and I lift a hand in return.

The last time I took the elevator I ran into one of my class-mates, so I opt for the stairs instead. On the third floor, I take two rights and a left, and end up in the long-term-care ward. Room 222B. A quick tap on the door, and George calls a gruff greeting to enter.

His leg must be bothering him today. He is resting in bed instead of in the chair by the window. Pain creases his face into a tic-tac-toe grid of wrinkles. The flourescent lights are not kind. Every age spot and puckered scar is visible, as if I've used a 50mm f/1.8 lens to take his picture. George doesn't give a shit about things like that, though. That's why he's my favorite subject to photograph.

"Hey, George."

Something sparks, and the deep grooves in his face smooth out a little. We never discuss how much we enjoy these visits. At least, not to each other. He doesn't quite smile, but I know he is happy. "Hey there, Sophie. What the hell are you doin' here on a Sunday?"

Because George does, everyone here calls me Sophie. He throws his left leg over the edge of the bed. From the knee down, an empty space occupies the area where his right leg should be.

I wanted to see a friendly face. "That's a nice way to greet a girl, George. No wonder Nurse Espinoza won't give you the time of day." Well, that, plus she is half his age, the old geezer.

He grins. "Shows what you know. The hussy was flirting with me not ten minutes ago."

I shake my head at his outright lie and drop my bag on the end of his bed. In an orchestrated dance, I step slightly in front of George and to the right so he can hold on to my shoulder. I am the only one he will accept help from in this way. Anyone else he would beat over the head with his crutch. He stands, balancing himself on one leg, and leans on my shoulder. The wheelchair is waiting when he twists sideways and seats himself. He grabs for my bag, and I place it in his lap, along with his coat. Without asking, he reaches into the bag for the digital camera. His camera, though he has loaned it to me indefinitely. Uncle Eddy's camera died a long time ago.

I push his wheelchair past the crowded atrium where all the weekenders go for family visitation. It's easier to hang out with the patients in the indoor garden, with its sunlight and picnic tables. Easier to forget that someone's ill when you're not surrounded by the antiseptic reek of hospital-issue debris. George and me, we don't like crowds, so we head outside, past the smokers in their hospital robes and nonskid socks. We follow the sidewalk to a small wooded area just off the parking lot. I stop George's chair at the edge of a melting snow bank, locking the brake so it won't roll down the incline.

George is already framing the first shot as I circle the chair. He starts clicking away, and I wander several feet, knowing he has already forgotten me with the camera in his hand.

Retired Sergeant First Class George Wilkins left the US Army after two tours in Vietnam. Then he returned for a third tour, only that time he shot his way through the country with a camera instead of a gun. A lot of the famous pictures I've seen in the old *Life* magazines are his. He considered it his job to create a visual record of the war, so people couldn't forget what his men—his brothers—had gone through.

We first met the day I got kicked off the cheer squad, when

my father ordered me to work at the VA Hospital after school a few days a week. He thought it would fill my time and keep me from bringing further dishonor to our family. I wonder how much shame people can hold before they ignite. If someone strikes a match to me, I think I will explode.

"Sophie?"

I hitch my chin in George's direction, and he snaps my picture. Tucking my hands deeper in my pockets, I fake a smile.

He frowns and lowers the camera. "What's wrong, girl? Your father giving you a hard time again?"

George thinks my father is a hard-ass and has offered to tell him so on occasion, but I haven't taken him up on it yet. I open my mouth to say I'm okay, to change the subject, to tell him anything except the truth.

He gives me his "don't fuck with me, kid" look.

I wish I could hide under my bedspread again, where nobody can see the tears I have to blink away.

George unlocks the brake on his chair and rolls closer. Concern pleats the skin of his forehead. He points to the weathered picnic table that's used by hospital employees to catch a smoke between shifts. I push him toward the table, glad for the moment to compose myself. I'm almost okay when I sit facing him.

Then he touches my chin, forcing me to meet his hazy gray gaze.

It's like the gesture gives my tear ducts permission to let loose.

"Talk to me," he says.

I hiccup through a laugh that's one part bitter and two parts terror. "Carey. He's MIA."

"Fuck."

George pats my arm. That's all it takes to send me over the edge. I'm laughing and crying in a squelchy mess. And then I'm just crying while George holds my hand, and I hate myself for wishing for a second that I'd never met Carey. That I'd never fallen for him—or taken the fall for him.

"Can I offer you some advice, Sophie?" George asks.

He sounds hesitant, very un-George-like, and he retrieves his hand when I nod. My coat sleeve is soaked from scrubbing my face like a five-year-old.

"Stop protecting them. They're grown men. You're not doing anyone any favors, least of all yourself, girl."

Them? I've told George next to nothing about my life outside this hospital. We mostly talk about the Veterans History Project. It's my job to help him collect stories, photos, and mementos from soldiers who want their military memories to live on at the Library of Congress. I'm continuing George's mission to keep a record of war. This place—my time with him—it's where I forget everything that came before.

"What makes you think I'm protecting anyone?"

He snorts. "Only someone with their head up their ass would think you betrayed that boy. I'd known you five minutes when I knew what kind of person you are. And no way in hell are you a lying cheat like they say," he says, nodding his head toward the hospital.

I freeze. "They talk about me in there?"

A shrug and another snort. "Only the people from around Sweethaven. We're sitting ducks for gossip, Soph, and your dad is well known around here. Besides, what else do we have to do? Play hopscotch?"

I should have guessed the gossip would follow me here. My dad is the reason I work at the hospital in the first place. I'm not upset like I thought I'd be, though. A tiny spark of warmth kindles inside me. Because George heard the awful things people say about me and doesn't believe them. I think he must be the only one. One in a million.

George's peppered hair covers the bald spot on the top of his head in a combover. Despite everything, my lips slip into a smile. "Liar," I say. "Everyone knows you sneak into the atrium to play poker with the guys from 216C."

"Son of a bitch, you say."

A breeze sweeps through the ash trees, and the bare branches sway. George hides a shiver. The past weeks have brought fragility to him that he won't acknowledge. I rise and circle the chair to push him back toward the hospital.

We are silent until I ask, "George?"

"Hmph?"

"Thanks for not believing the gossip."

He reaches back to pat my hand with his wrinkled one.

Chapter Five

Monday means school, and school means tarring-and-feathering for the slutty girl who cheated on her saintly boyfriend. Like their parents, my classmates believe I've broken the code. *Didn't you hear? She was fucking some other guy before Carey even left for Afghanistan.*

I'd hate that girl too, if I didn't know the truth about her. And it doesn't really matter how good or kind she was before.

I wait until the last bell rings before I enter the school. Better to be tardy than brave the crowded halls alone. That is a lesson I learned the hard way.

After the photo was first posted, I grew accustomed to the stares. My classmates and I have come to an uneasy truce. I don't speak to them, and they pretend I don't exist. It works with everyone, except Jamie. With Carey out of the way, she's made it her mission to destroy me. I want to tell her to give it up: Carey can't love her no matter how hard she tries. But that would lead to questions and explanations I can't give.

Whatever progress I've made in the six months since Jamie posted the picture of me on the Web will have been destroyed by the latest news about Carey. The scene at Bob's proved that.

Yellow ribbons are plastered on many of the orange lockers in the deserted main hallway. I hadn't expected that, but it doesn't surprise me a bit. Carey is ours. He might as well have a PROPERTY OF SWEETHAVEN label stamped on his ass. He belongs to this town, and we belong to him. These ribbons say *I'm proud of you* and *I miss you* and *Come home safe*. I feel a twinge of fierce longing and love for my former friends.

Then I arrive at my locker to retrieve my calculus book for first period. The artist really took his or her time carving TRAITOR into the metal skin of my locker. And beneath that, in larger letters: WHORE. They must have used an awl because the letters are good and deep. The message will reappear like magic no matter how many coats of paint Mr. Dupree, the janitor, slaps on it.

Freaking awesome.

You'd think they could find a scrap of originality after all these months.

It sucked to start my senior year crowned as the town slut.

News traveled fast in our town of 3,053, and the night before school started, a picture hit the Internet and lit our corner of the world on fire. Some had a "don't ask, don't tell" policy about cheating, and the appearance of my half-naked self on Facebook challenged that. The picture had to have been taken by accident. Shot from the end zone at an August football scrimmage, the foreground featured our team celebrating on the sidelines of a rival school's field. Blake and I were only noticeable upon closer scrutiny, hidden as we were behind the bleachers.

Lucky for him, the shadows obscured almost everything that could reveal his identity, except for a small tattoo on his lower back that nobody knew he had, except Carey and me. My identity, on the other hand, couldn't have been clearer. Standing in my cheer skirt and a lacy bra, I'd wrapped myself around Blake's naked torso. The amateur photographer had accidentally struck PG–13 gold when they'd captured that shot.

Most people remembered Carey had been at that game just before he shipped out. The fact that I would cheat while he was there at the game, days before he went to war for our country, only added to my reputation.

The comments on my Facebook profile, the crank calls, and the nasty e-mails had started up as soon as the picture hit the Internet. I'd thought they'd prepared me to go to school the next day, but then the call had come from the school office Sunday evening. My father and I had received a summons to see the principal first thing in the morning, but my father had already gone off on a fishing trip.

So I'd waited until the last possible minute to drive myself to school. I'd taken a deep breath and plunged through Sweethaven

High's double doors with my head held high, hoping the hall would be empty, even though I'd mentally prepared myself to be shunned. I might as well have a KICK ME sign taped to my back. Nobody would see the war paint I'd chosen—"Marine Green" nail polish for my toes—but Carey would've liked it. Too bad he'd already been in the desert for a few weeks.

You've done nothing wrong. The school doors swung closed behind me, and everyone stared at my cheerleading uniform with QUINN embroidered on the left breast of the scratchy wool sweater—my version of giving them all the bird while I quaked to Reese's Pieces inside. Carey's Quinn could weather the scorn. I'd promised.

My friends had crammed into the hall, along with those who wanted to witness my downfall. As Carey's girlfriend, I'd become Somebody. I'd transformed from tomboy into cheerleader, shedding the strangled mop of hair and losing the braces. Looking more like my mother and less like a scrawny ragamuffin helped, too. But things changed that first day of school. My classmates' whispers hushed, and they froze like cockroaches do when you flip on the bathroom light in the middle of the night. Surprised. Busted.

I spotted Nikki and Angel in the crowd. They'd kept our summer pact to go blond, and Nikki's natural red color tinted her hair the brass of Elliot Morgan's tuba. Angel could have been Marilyn Monroe's younger sister. I'd forgotten how I'd obsessed over damaging my black hair by bleaching it blond. I hadn't wanted to disappoint my friends by backing out. Now my long black hair seemed to say, *One of these things is not like the others.*

A small part of me believed they would stand by me. Cheer sisters. Beer sisters. Each of us a third of a best-friends charm. We'd helped one another through acne, first kisses, and cheer tryouts. Maybe that meant something. Months before, at Carey's party, Angel had promised they would be there for me.

For an instant, Angel's eyes flickered with worry, but it was too fast to be sure. The two of them flipped their pleated cheer skirts in disdain as they turned their twin letterman jackets on me. Carey's Quinn faltered.

I'd known how it would be: Guilty until Carey proved me innocent. You didn't cheat on the hometown hero and expect a welcoming parade. I couldn't have guessed how my stomach would bottom out. The urge to tell crawled up the back of my throat.

Move your damned feet, Quinn.

Answering the summons to the principal's office, I headed for the door at the opposite end of the long hallway, ignoring Josh Danvers when he stepped too close, his linebacker's shoulders thrown back in a show of solidarity for Carey. They'd played football and been in ROTC together before Carey had graduated early.

My breath skipped.

Shoving past Josh, I focused on the dingy gray door of the main office, determined to make it to that temporary refuge before my courage split for Canada.

Someone shouted, "Slut!"

My face burned, and several people laughed. I would not cry, would not cry, would not cry. The desire to hide pushed me forward. One step. And then another.

I used to be like them, but then Jamie sending that picture changed everything. I don't know if she was the one to take the photo, but she'd been quick to capitalize on it. Last night I'd e-mailed Carey before his parents could. Before Jamie could gleefully tell him what I'd done in her bitchy efforts to break us up.

For once, he wrote back within hours. *Everything will be okay*—rememberyourpromise—*we'll figure something out.*

Then the phone calls started, with whispered accusations of *WhoresluttrampTRAITOR*. After the tenth venomous e-mail, I'd shut my laptop and hoped this would go away. Lying awake in my bed, I told myself to be ready for the smear campaign. For the first time since reading *The Scarlet Letter*, I sympathized with the adulterous Hester.

And as I stood in the hallway that day, I guessed I would hear the whispers for some time to come.

WhoresluttrampTRAITOR.

The office door blurred as my eyes strained with the effort of holding back tears. Not one of my friends had asked for my side of the story. My *friends* had abandoned me. I wanted to shove a scarlet letter down each of their throats.

"Call me Hester Prynne," I muttered, twisting the familiar chain of my necklace around my fingers like a talisman.

There was no looking back. I entered the office.

And now that Carey's missing, I am back at square one.

Calculus sucks. English bites. Third-period Spanish completely blows chunks. Saturday at Bob's was just the start of things to come. Jamie has fired everyone up into rare form.

Two collisions send my books flying and a shove pushes me into a row of lockers. I never see the culprits. They hide in the crowd. I guess I expected the boys to be awful with their macho, stand-by-our-man posturing. The girls are worse, though. Crueler.

A single seat is left open for me in my fourth-period physics class. *Yeah, like that wasn't planned.* Jamie, Nikki, and Angel form a horseshoe around my desk. Jamie's brown eyes are dark with promised retribution. She's always wanted Carey, which means she'd like a truck to take me out while I'm crossing the street. Unlike Nikki and Angel, she is neither blond, nor beautiful, nor a cheerleader. Oh no, she's our future valedictorian, class president, and yearbook editor. I'm fairly certain my picture won't be appearing in the yearbook this year.

It would be so much easier to hate Jamie if she were vapid, but she's not. Instead, she is that niggling voice in my head. The one that points out everything I've done wrong and all the people I've let down during these past few months.

I slide into the empty seat, dropping my book bag onto the floor. Mr. Brolley starts a lecture on the laws of thermodynamics. Out of the corner of my eye, I see Jamie shoot Nikki a glance, one brunette brow arching as she tilts her head toward me. *Here we go.*

Nikki starts the game by throwing a pen at my head. Every time Mr. Brolley turns his back, Jamie or Nikki pulls my ponytail, kicks my chair, or mutters a curse under her breath. Childish, but effective. Others notice but say nothing.

I lose it.

As Jamie reaches for me again, I block her with a vicious swing of my forearm.

"Bitch!" she hisses, cradling her arm.

I smile and resume taking notes.

School should not be this hard, but at least none of them bother me for the rest of the period.

The bell rings.

Jamie hits me with her bag as she walks by, and I almost go after her. A hand on my shoulder stays me.

"Don't, Q," Angel whispers. "It'll only make things worse."

She's spent the past hour watching them harass me, and she didn't say a word. I can't help wondering why she cares. "Since when did you become her minion, Ang?"

She shrugs. "It's not like that. Besides, Jamie's not so bad."

That's not what you used to say. I shove my books into my bag and rise. "She's horrible. I can't believe you don't see that."

Gathering her faded blond waves into an impromptu ponytail, Angel frowns. "And you cheated on Carey before he even left."

Sudden longing fills me. I miss her. I want one friend to know I'm not guilty of that crime. To have just one person on my side. Carey can't blame me for that, right?

I touch her arm, and she pauses. Our eyes meet, and in that instant I know Ang would keep my secret—Carey's secret. She'd hug me and tell me she's sorry. Lunch, weekends; I wouldn't have to be alone anymore.

Angel gives me a questioning glance, and I want her friendship again so badly that my guts twist with it.

"I wish things were different," I say instead.

She shrugs again. "Me too."

I let her go to catch up with Jamie. I am spineless. If I tell Ang the truth, she would be punished right along with me, assuming her parents even let her hang with me—her mother is a Marine deployed in Iraq, and I've betrayed the code.

Jamie spares me another glare from the door, and I wonder if she got someone to deface my locker or if she did it herself.

WhoresluttrampTRAITOR.

No. I won't drag another person down into this hell.

Chapter Six

Lunch is an awfully big adventure.

Before Carey left, we used to eat lunch in the cafeteria. When he went off to basic training, I ate with the cheer squad. Last September, though, I started brown-bagging it when I realized the cafeteria offered nothing but humiliation. The attention faded in October when Coach Jorgenson busted Mark Harrison with a nickel bag in his locker. The gossip mill chewed on him for a while. I've been wallpaper ever since.

But Carey going missing has put me back in the public eye.

I think longingly of going home to eat, but Principal Barkley had put the kibosh on students leaving campus for lunch after too many seniors ditched their afternoon classes. Which means everyone's in the cafeteria. I consider hiding in the library, but Mrs. Hall, the librarian I've known since I was seven, shooed me out without any sympathy. Her husband served under my father.

Entering the cafeteria with its predictable smells (french fries on Mondays, pizza on Tuesdays, mystery meat on Wednesdays, and so on), I twist the chain of my necklace around my fingers and search for a seat away from the crowd. I wait a heartbeat too long.

"You have nerve, Quinn."

Jamie blocks my path with one fist on her hip, like a model posing at the end of the runway. She takes up a lot of space for such an average girl. My body language says, *Anyone have a rock I can hide under?*

The room pops with confrontation. It's obvious I'm going to pay for defending myself in class.

Jamie's face glows with hatred and triumph. "I can't believe you still wear that." She gestures to the necklace tangled around my fingers. Carey's class ring dangles from it. "I noticed you weren't wearing it when you were screwing that other boy."

She holds up her phone, and I recognize the picture on the screen. She's blown it up, nice and big. Even after all this time, the photo humiliates me. My eyes burn. *Damn you; don't you dare cry.*

Jamie pretends to study it. "You might want to think about working out, Quinnie. Looks like you've put on some weight."

I can see my future before me in that moment. This—*this* shitty moment—will be every day of my senior year as long as Carey is missing. Repeated over and over again in a thousand different ways. Because I promised him. I love Carey. I'm scared he won't be found. I'm terrified he won't be found alive. So even though it sucks, I suck it up. The sick rolls in my stomach, but I not about to let Jamie break me.

She pushes into my space, a whole six inches taller than my five-foot-one-inch frame. "Who's in the picture with you?"

This has bothered her for months. She has harped on it. She thought I would spill my guts when the pictures hit the Internet. The more she tries to get a confession out of me, the tighter I close my lips to spite her. Besides, Blake is right. It would only hurt the Breens to admit I'd been kissing him.

Jamie pushes again. "Come on, Quinn. Who was it?"

My mouth opens, as if pulled by her demands.

That's when Blake steps forward. He doesn't have to do anything more to command attention. Carey and Blake acted like brothers, but while Carey's lips tip into quick smiles, Blake waits. I can't think of another way to describe it. I can never tell what he is thinking. Jamie clearly can't either, and she backs off in a hurry, watching to see what he'll do.

"Tell them," Blake says.

His quiet voice rumbles through the cafeteria like slow thunder. This is the first time he has confronted me in public since the pictures came out. Carey's best friend confronting the whore girlfriend.

They don't hear what I do in his words. They are a dare and a plea. Something's happened since we talked Saturday. Some part of him wants me to tell the truth, so he can be punished along-side me. I'm almost selfish enough to do it. Except then I would be blamed for his downfall—nobody ever faults the boy—and besides, I still have lingering feelings for him despite my best efforts.

So I repeat his words from Saturday. "Fuck you." *Fuck you for trying to make me confess for you.* I survey the cafeteria. "That goes for all of you. I don't owe any of you a thing."

When I try to walk away, Jamie grabs my arm, her nails digging into my flesh. "You don't deserve Carey. You—"

"Don't you get it, Jamie?" I shake my head in disbelief. "None of this matters. He's missing, and you're worried about some stupid picture that he already knows about."

Blake's head snaps toward me. I hadn't told him that Carey knew about the picture. I'm sure he's wondering if Carey figured out Blake's the one with his hand on my breast, but I'm not about to tell him. It's revengeful and petty, and I can't believe how good it feels.

"Fuck with my locker all you want. I don't really give a shit."

Jamie tenses. I've guessed right. She was behind the damage. Her nails sink deeper into my forearm, threatening to cut my skin. I start to shove her away when Mrs. Breen calls my name.

"Quinn. Principal Barkley's office. Now."

Carey's mother. Just fuck.

In September, on that first day at school, when I entered the principal's office, Principal Barkley's secretary had given me a sharp look. The heavy woman bore a strong resemblance to a marshmallow and, on most days, her personality could be just as sweet. But she'd clearly heard the rumors, and her soft body shivered with disapproval like an overweight terrier when she saw me.

"Ted, the Quinn girl is here." She said into the phone. While she paused to listen, I had wondered if I would be referred to as "the Quinn girl" by every adult who looked down his or her nose at me. Mrs. Rodriguez set the receiver in its cradle and said in a snotty tone, "Go in. Principal Barkley is waiting on you."

The only other time I'd been to Barkley's office had been before the photo leaked. He'd stood to open the door and ushered me in with a cheerful smile. He'd asked about cheerleading, my dad, and Carey. Because in Sweethaven, even the high school principal knew I'd been dating Carey for two years and was going on marriage and 2.5 kids in a house on Do-What's-Expected Street.

Things had changed, though. Principal Barkley had two sons serving in Iraq, and he'd served in Desert Storm before them.

Barkley didn't bother to rise from his chair when I entered, and he also didn't offer me a seat. Instead, when I started to close the door, he gestured for me to keep it open. As if I would make a pass at him. As if a middle-aged man with a bald spot the size of Texas and a bushy gray beard made my knees quake. My hands tugged down the hem of my cheer skirt, and I prayed the visit would end quickly.

Barkley adjusted his ugly tie and cleared his throat.

"Sophie—"

"It's Quinn."

"Right. Quinn."

He folded his hands on top of a file that probably contained a copy of the incriminating photo. My shame in a manila folder. I felt my cheeks burn at the idea that Barkley had seen it, had studied it while deciding whether or not to expel me. Had it given him a cheap thrill?

"Quinn, I think you know why you're here. You—"

"No," I interrupted. I'm not sure why I did it, except that I hated how smug he looked.

"I'm sorry?"

Principal Barkley's confusion acted as a balm to the ache in my belly. "I said, no. I have no idea why I'm here."

For a single moment, he hesitated. His pompous mask slipped as he tried to figure out if I was screwing with him.

"A . . . compromising . . . picture of you and another boy was e-mailed to members of the school board this morning."

A moan almost escaped, but I crushed my lips together in time.

Barkley continued. "I've been trying to reach your father. I think it's vital we all get on the same page before this gets out of control." He tugged on his tie again.

"He left yesterday on a fishing trip with Reverend Cooper," I admitted. "His phone doesn't always work up at the lake." Only that morning I'd still hoped there was a chance this would blow past without him ever finding out.

Barkley cleared his throat again. "Yes, well. Considering his unavailability, I think we can reconvene this discussion when we are able to reach him. Until then, I'd like you to go to class."

My father would kill me.

Knuckles rapped on the door, and Mrs. Breen's voice sounded behind me. "I have a question, Quinn."

Carey's mother was Sweethaven's cheer coach and a den mother to the team. More to me. The most painful thing about keeping Carey's secret was losing his parents. Every time I had had a crisis, I'd headed to the Breens. When my mother left, Mrs. Breen ran her fingers through my hair while I cried in her lap. When my father forgot my fifteenth birthday, Mr. Breen ran to the store for a cake and lame party hats. *I'm sorry, Quinnie,* he'd told me with a crooked grin. *It was Power Rangers or Barbie, and you've always struck me as a kickass kind of girl.*

Mrs. Breen's brown eyes, so similar to Carey's, were bloodshot, as if she'd been crying. If anyone could have made me confess the truth, it was her. The words climbed back up my throat, but the white lines around her mouth stopped me. Carey had been the first to point out that those lines were a litmus test, proof-positive of rage.

"How could you, Quinn? Carey's barely been in Afghanistan a few weeks. When he finds out—"

"He knows," I said.

"What?" Her voice dropped to a near whisper at my words.

"Carey knows."

She wanted to slap me. I could see her hand itching with the urge. She gathered herself.

"If he dies, I won't forgive you." She paused. "You're off the team, Quinn. What you did—the picture—you signed a contract when you joined the squad. To be an example for the other kids. I think we can agree that no parent wants their child following your example."

WhoresluttrampTRAITOR.

Her words were worse than a slap. My head bowed.

"Please go to the locker room and change out of your uniform."

Barkley said nothing. I rose and turned to leave without making eye contact. Carey's mother touched my arm when I passed. I looked up, hoping . . .

"Who's the boy, Quinn?" she pleaded.

Sometimes a moment defines you, defines how people see you the rest of your life. That's something my father said, a truism he shared with his troops. *You can accept it or fight it. If you're lucky, you'll recognize the moment when it happens.*

This was my moment. I could name the boy. I could tell the truth, but it wouldn't do any good. Everyone had made their minds up. Only Carey could save me, and he wasn't here. A promise was a promise.

I walked out of Barkley's office without a backward glance.

"I hope for your sake he was worth it."

The curse rang in my ears. Part of me couldn't blame her.

Starring in a photo wearing your lacy best with a half-naked boy draped across your front ranked pretty high on the list of Things Parents Frowned Upon. Having said photo spread like a virus on the Internet and to every mobile phone in a twenty-mile radius? A definite no-no. And what I did was ten times—a thousand times—worse, because the boy in that picture wasn't her son.

Carey didn't have a tattoo of a tiny bird on his left lower back, two inches beneath the waist of his pants. Blake did.

Chapter Seven

Principal Barkley's office looks the same as it did six months ago, and he doesn't mince words when I am in front of him.

"Some students have organized a candlelight vigil for Carey at Town Hall this evening."

Understandable. And most likely Jamie's doing. In our town, Marine families stick together. The vigil is less about Carey than about showing the Breens support. But I don't see why he would call me in to his office to tell me this. He must see my confusion, because he seems embarrassed.

"The Breens have asked that you not attend."

I swallow, give a jerky nod, and tilt my head to study his water-stained ceiling so I won't cry. Not here. Not in front of him.

After Barkley excuses me, I do not return to class. I head for the safety of my Jeep.

Blake is standing in the hall with Angel as I head for the exit, and I avoid their eyes.

"Q?"

Worry punches holes in Blake's usual bitter tone, but I ignore him. I don't stop until I am in my Jeep and pulling away from the school. It's only when I see my reflection in the rearview mirror that I realize I'm crying.

I'm not sure where to go. Home is out, since my father could show up there at any time. People in town would call the school to narc on me for ditching.

I drive to the northern side of Sweethaven. At the edge of Grave Woods, I pull off the road and into a copse of trees. My tires have worn grooves into the mud over the past couple of months. In seconds, I'm parked out of sight of anyone passing on the road. Safe. Lost.

George's Nikon somehow ends up in my hand, and I strip it of its case, tossing my bag of equipment over my shoulder. It's cold, but bearable, as I trek the half hour into the woods to the grave-yard. With only three graves and said to be haunted, the tiny plot is little more than a few mounds of melting snow bowing to long-forgotten headstones. Nobody knows who Josephine, Thomas, or Susie were, but it's obvious from the sad state of the stones that they died long ago. Somehow, I feel less alone when I come here.

Snow can be difficult to shoot, but those wasting piles, untouched by tires, are where I focus. If I'm not careful, the pictures will appear too dark or the snow will come out a shade of blue. The trick is to overexpose—to fool the camera into thinking there is more light than there really is.

Not so different from me. I've fooled everyone into thinking I'm more than I really am.

I adjust the ISO setting and use my exposure compensation dial. Then I linger like George has taught me. *Everyone takes the picture of the kid with the birthday cake on his face*, he said once. *Wait for the unexpected. That's the magic.*

So I crouch and I wait, expelling my breath into my scarf. My right calf cramps, and my hip clicks when I shift to ease the discomfort. It's silent, until something moves above me.

A crow perches on a branch a mere ten feet away, unaware it is a living, breathing graveyard cliché. I snap its picture and remember a nursery rhyme my mother used to lull me to sleep when a song could still do the trick.

One for sorrow, two for joy, three for a girl, four for a boy, five for silver, six for gold, seven for a secret never to be told.

The crow looses a shrill *"Ca-caw!"* that is answered in duplicate. Suddenly a murder of crows is launching out of the tree tops, their blue-black feathers flicking white powder into the air. My finger is fast on the trigger, shooting as many pictures as I can.

Unlike that rhyme, I don't believe the number of birds I see will determine my fate. But that doesn't stop me from counting them through the viewfinder as they wing away.

Seven. Seven for a secret never to be told.

* * *

Soon my fingers are cramping from the cold, and I pack up my gear. I've lost hours in the woods capturing the crows, a deer, the way the ice crystallizes on the trees, the ground flattened by my boots. I don't know if any of the pictures will be good, but sometimes I surprise myself.

The Jeep chugs to a start, and I pray the heater works. It finally kicks in when I pass Town Hall. There are people gathering outside the white clapboard building and pouring inside the huge oak doors.

Right. The candlelight vigil. I'd almost managed to forget about it. Perhaps that is the "magic of photography" that George describes.

No candles are lit, but the sun is only just beginning to set. As awful as they would treat me, I want to be inside that building. I want to sit on one of the long benches beside the Breens, listening to Carey's friends talk about him. But I am not welcome, so I keep driving, hoping I haven't been noticed.

I can't go home to sit alone in the dark. I belong nowhere. Nobody wants me.

That thought brings on a raspy laugh. Can I sound any sorrier for myself?

Honestly, there's only one place *to* go.

Twenty minutes of winding road later, I'm at the overlook. The last time I sat here, Carey and Blake were both beside me.

We were just us, and things hadn't blown all to hell.

Squinting down at Town Hall, I see they've lit the candles. Our school is small—only 429 students total—but a lot of the students will be down there, along with their parents. I can't make out the individual flickers, but hundreds of flames shimmer and burn together. It's beautiful and eerie and sad. My eyes never leave the sight as I climb out of the Jeep and pull myself up to sit on the warm hood.

Holding a vigil feels like we are saying good-bye. Giving up on Carey. I wish I could talk to him right now. Not to hash out what happened before he left, just to be with him. Wherever he is, if he is able to, he is worrying about me, Blake, and his parents. It's his way. I squeeze my eyes closed. *Carey, Carey, Carey.* I think the words like a prayer. If I am fierce enough, maybe God will return my best friend.

"I miss you, Carey," I whisper.

"Do you think he misses you, Q?"

The voice startles me, and I nearly fall off my perch. Angel stands beside my Jeep, shifting awkwardly from one foot to the other. Her car is parked behind mine on the shoulder, though I didn't hear her arrive.

She dangles a six-pack of beer from her forefinger. "Mind if I join you?"

It could be any Saturday night from our past. Out of habit, I shrug, and she passes me the beer so she can hoist herself up next to me. She retrieves the six-pack and offers me one. I take it and crack the top, not because I want it, but because it's the first thing she has offered me in months.

Sipping from her can, Angel studies the town below. The moon is bright, and her makeup has faded enough to reveal a pink zit on her chin. Her blond hair is tucked under a ski cap, and she looks like my old friend, the one I bumped hips with at a party almost a year ago.

"You didn't answer my question."

I hesitate, picking my words with care. "Yes. He misses me."

She tilts her head back and shoots me a knowing look. "You've talked to him."

It's not a question, but I nod. There's a long pause as she studies me. I'm not sure what she sees before she turns back to the town. Silence falls, and it is the uncomfortable kind I hate.

When I can't stand it any longer, I blurt out, "Why aren't you down there with everyone else?"

It's her turn to shrug. "It's the Jamie Show down there. Carey didn't particularly like her, so it didn't seem right to . . ."

She drifts off. I get that. I've been drifting for months. We sip our beers.

"We all thought you would get married. Nikki and I had a bet going that he would propose before he left."

I say nothing.

"It should be you down there, Q. Comforting his parents. Helping Blake hold it together."

Her eyes are narrowed in accusation.

What is there to say besides "I know, Ang."

My admission is not enough for her. She slides to her feet and faces me. "Then why aren't you?"

I shake my head. My fingers quiver around the cold can, and I want to answer her so badly. She steps forward and touches my foot, nudging it gently.

"It's not that easy," I say helplessly.

Any secret I tell her, she will be forced to keep. As shitty as the last year has been, I don't want her to share in the hatred toward me, especially now that it's been reignited with Carey's disappearance. It wouldn't be fair. Not to her.

Disappointment replaces the hope that widened her eyes. Her hand falls from my foot, and she walks away, leaving the beer behind.

"Ang?" I call to her. "I'm not a whore. You know me better than that."

That's it. My only defense. The only truth I can say.

Her steps never falter. She doesn't believe me. I've lost my chance. Her car's headlights temporarily blind me as she leaves.

I'm alone. Again.

Chapter Eight

I should have guessed Carey was gay.

At least that's what I tell myself in hindsight, but his brilliance blinded me. The way he cared for everyone around him with this huge, open heart. How he could tease anyone—even my father—into smiling.

When we first started dating, we kissed. We made out in Grave Woods. At my house, at his house, walking between our houses. And when he got his license, we took our lips to the overlook like all the other couples.

It's screwed up how I thought we would always be together, but I never questioned why his arms cradled me without heat. His hands did not test my will or pull at the zipper of my jeans. His fingers did not trace my ribs up, up, up until bone gave way to breast.

What kind of boyfriend doesn't try to race the bases? What kind of girlfriend doesn't care? I thought, *He loves me. He respects me.*

We're taking our time because we have all the time in the world.

And then his early graduation snuck up on us. He enlisted in the Marines in January, his years of ROTC and physical training finally paying off. Basic training and SOI—the School of Infantry—commanded his focus for months, while I finished up my junior year. Then there was that short visit in May, and waiting and waiting for his leave in August. The wondering if he'd propose before he deployed. Pride. Worry. Fear. An unnamed twist in my gut. My emotions *tick-tick-tick*ing like the timer on a bomb counting down to desperation.

So I pushed him. The night he came home during his last leave, I stood back while he greeted his family. Waves of pride poured off his father and spilled onto everyone. We watched him hug Carey, who looked handsome and strange in his uniform. His mother's smile reminded me of a snagged sweater. Pull the loose thread and the whole thing would unravel. She hadn't wanted Carey to enlist, but she was doing her best to keep it together since he was getting deployed.

After dinner, when the Breens were finally tired, Carey drove me home and we sat on our porch swing. I lay with my head on his lap, his thigh muscles shifting beneath me with every lazy push. His fingers toyed with the thin strap of my dress, caressing my shoulder. My father had stayed overnight on base since they needed him for training exercises in the morning. The only company Carey and I had were the cicadas rattling like a thousand rusty watches being wound.

Turning my head, I studied Carey, trying to discover how he had changed. Some differences I had noticed in May: The hair, of course, buzzed, and unveiling a smattering of freckles on his scalp. His posture had changed, too. His shoulders were now straight and squared, like my father's. But more than just his physical appearance had transformed over the summer.

Reaching up, I touched his cheek, trailing my fingers across his whiskers, and when his eyes met mine, I saw it—that thing that had bothered me since we had picked him up at the airport. The thing I hadn't wanted to notice in May: Distance. Even as his body touched mine, I couldn't feel him.

"What's wrong?" I whispered.

The void between us widened when he grasped my hand, casually placing it back on my stomach. I sat up, letting my feet fall to the porch.

"Carey?"

He reacted to the tremor in my voice. The muscles in his face worked as his jaw clenched to hold back whatever words were trying to escape. He rarely withheld the truth, and suddenly I thought of ten things horrible enough for him to want to protect me. Most of them centered on where he was going in a couple of weeks and if he would come back.

"I have something to tell you, Quinn. Don't freak out, okay?"

I hesitated, waiting.

He rubbed both palms on his jeans. "Geez, this is hard."

The swing jerked beneath me when he rose, and I grabbed

for the chain to keep my balance. I pulled my knees up to my chest, wrapping my arms around them. Carey didn't pace. In control of his body, if not his emotions, he walked to the edge of the porch and leaned against the railing, putting a mile of space between us.

A bead of sweat trickled in an S curve from his forehead to his cheek, and I eyed him with worry.

"You know I love you, right, Quinn?"

He cheated on me, I thought. *He didn't want me anymore, and this was his way of telling me.* I couldn't take the stalling. "Just say it already."

His hand rasped over his head, and he tucked his arms over his chest like he did when he was nervous.

"I'm gay." He expelled the words on a long sigh.

I froze. *No, no, no. Hell no.*

His eyes locked on my face, searching. Everything in me wanted to reject his words, and I could see he knew it by the way his lips pressed together. So I shut down, clamping down tight on any emotion so I wouldn't make a fool of myself. Because for one tiny moment, when I thought he might confess he'd cheated, I'd mostly felt relief. And because somehow his news wasn't unexpected.

"Say something," he whispered.

Like what? How could I tell him the things running through my head? *It's my fault. How long has he known? Why now? Why is he telling me now? Has he met someone? Who else knows? How could he love me and still be gay?* Because I didn't doubt he loved me.

"You're freaking out, aren't you?"

"I'm . . . thinking." And I was. My mind raced through conversations and kisses, trying to figure out how I could have been so stupid. Two years we'd been together and never once had sex, or even come close to it. Why did I think that was normal? All our time together, and he'd never wanted me. And what about me? Why hadn't I pushed harder?

"You lied to me." I winced when I heard my voice sounding tiny and pathetic. Worse, I started crying.

"Shit. I should've kept my mouth shut," he said, and I heard, *I thought about not telling you.*

"Have you met someone?" I asked, and instantly I could see he had.

Guilt. From the tips of his red ears to the white lines at the corners of his mouth pinched into a grimace, he looked guilty. He shrugged.

"Geez, you're an asshole, Carey. You were really going to leave me here waiting for you?"

He'd considered leaving me here, pining after him, not knowing the truth, waiting for him while he risked his life overseas. Something had changed his mind, though.

"I'd thought about it, but I couldn't do that to you." He crouched down, his thigh muscles shifting from the strain as he balanced on the balls of his feet. "I'm sorry. I didn't want this. I fought against it for so long. Hoping I could be . . . normal."

Honesty. Pain. Shame. His emotions battered me, leaving no space for me to breathe, and through it all, he kept watching me, his brown eyes terrified.

"I didn't want to be different. Not like this."

Then he was crying too. I choked out sobs, torn between wanting to comfort my best friend and feeling betrayed by his sadness when *I* was the hurt one.

My stomach heaved, picturing him kissing another guy like he'd never kissed me.

I ran for the screen door, but his arms encircled me from behind, pulling me back against his chest.

"Quinn, please," he begged. "I'm so sorry. Don't go."

For one moment, I let him hold me. And then I remembered the first time he kissed me. *I won't ever let you down.*

"No!" I fought him until he let me go, then whipped around to glare at him. Tears tracked down his cheeks, but I didn't care. He reached for me again, and I shoved him as hard as I could.

"Get the fuck away from me, Carey."

He didn't try to stop me again.

I went into the house, closing and locking the front door behind me. It took ten minutes—ten agonizing minutes— before I heard his boots scrape across the porch and his car drive away.

Two hours after that, I backed my Jeep out of the driveway, knowing I needed to get away but unsure where I was going until I ended up parked outside Blake's house.

In the days after the candlelight vigil, I am stoic. My classmates can't hurt me worse than they already have. I carry my books in my backpack and avoid my locker and any nasty surprises it might contain. I arrive early to class so I can pick a rear seat where I can put my back to the wall and nobody can fuck with me. The whispers are easier to blast out with earbuds and loud music on my iPod. When they shove me or trip me, I pick myself up and move on. Blake doesn't exist when I keep my eyes straight ahead and my focus on praying for Carey's return.

I know life here is not the norm. But in our town, there are three classes—poor, middle, and Marine. When money runs in short supply, so do your options. You want to go to college? Then you'd better enlist to get your education paid for. You don't want to go to college? Then you'd better enlist to learn a trade that can get you out of Sweethaven. Otherwise, you'll end up slinging pancakes at the diner.

My entire life, I've watched the people of Sweethaven rally around one another, banding together, feeding one another, and sometimes, when things get really bad, taking one another in. The military is the backbone of our community, helping us to stand tall. Giving us pride because our men and women are serving our country.

But to be a part of our military town, you have to pay a price.

In the past twenty years, we've lost twenty soldiers in the Middle East. Others returned, not as they were, but as strangers.

And then there are the rules. I am not the first in our town to be caught cheating. A lot of ugly crap happens during the months that Marines are deployed. But I am the first in our high school.

Sometimes I think my friends—whose own parents have been deployed for months at a time—are taking their rage out on me. After all, why do they care about what happened between Carey and me? Then I remember how hard our town and its families have struggled to keep it together, and I forgive my friends a little because they don't know the truth.

My mom and I had struggled to hold it together too, while my father fought in Iraq. But she betrayed us. She changed our family forever with one selfish act. Now it looks like I've betrayed Carey in the worst way.

Maybe I would want to destroy me too.

Chapter Nine

George cheats at games.

His eyes stray toward my cards, and I angle my hand closer to my chest, glaring at him. "Go fish."

He takes a card off the top of the deck on the table and frowns. More than just about anything, he hates to lose, and I have to watch him closely so cards don't stray up his sleeve or under the blanket on his lap.

"Do you have a nine?"

His brow smoothes out, and he gives me an angelic smile. "Go fish, Soph."

I know he's lying and he knows I know he's lying. I raise an eyebrow at him. "Seriously, George? You're gonna play it like that?"

"Like what?" he asks, all innocence.

"We're not even betting money on this."

He tilts his head toward the fun-size candy bars piled on his bedside tray. "Those things are currency around here. Now shut up and draw, kid."

Placing my elbows on the tabletop, I lean forward until my face is in his. "Swear on your Cubans that you don't have a nine." I'm not sure how he gets them, but George has a steady supply of Cuban cigars. He loves them, but obviously not as much as he loves winning.

"I swear," he says, solemnly placing a hand over his heart.

He manages to hold my gaze for all of five seconds before his eyes drop. As soon as he looks away I steal at glance at his hand. Not only does he have a nine, he also has an ace and a queen he told me he didn't have.

"You lie like a dog, George. Give me the nine, and while you're at it, give me that ace and the queen."

Caught, he grins shamelessly and passes me the cards without argument. He groans when I smack down three pairs, finishing off my hand and pulling all the candy toward me.

"I win!" I crow. "That makes five hands, right?"

"Four." He crosses his arms while I do a miniature victory lap around his room. He's scowling, but doing a bad job at hiding a smile. "All right, smart-ass. Quit being a poor winner and hand me those photos."

The pictures are part of the Veterans History Project we've been working on since we met last year. We're helping Private Don Baruth in room 309 compile his mementos from his days fighting in the Korean War as part of the Army's 8th Calvary, 1st Calvary Division. Each piece of memorabilia has to be documented and Don's story has to be written up before we can submit his collection to the Library of Congress.

I drop the pictures onto George's lap and resume my seat on the side of the bed where his leg should be. It used to bother me, that missing leg.

"This one is amazing," I say, pulling a photo from the pile.

George studies it. The black-and-white shot features only a dirty helmet and the arm of an unseen soldier. George traces the arm, lost in memory. The images do this to him often, taking him back in time to things he'd rather forget and doesn't like to talk about.

"It's of a North Korean soldier Don had just shot in a skirmish along the Nakdong River, near Chingu."

The soldier is dead. Peering closer, I see the ground is a mixture of mud and what has to be blood. I hadn't realized. I picture Don as I'd seen him the week before. In his eighties, at least, he has more liver spots than hair. His skin sags with the weight of age, and his hands shook when he patted my arm to thank me for bringing him a cup of water.

"Why did he keep it? That seems a little creepy."

"He didn't want to forget how awful it felt to kill someone."

I say nothing. I can't imagine what it would be like to kill another human being. Someone who had a family who loved them. Somebody's son and maybe somebody's father. I wonder if Carey has had to kill anyone. Or worse, has someone killed Carey? I shiver, though it's not cold.

George sighs and takes a deep breath to pull himself back to the present. "Why do you think this photo is amazing?"

I pause, studying the picture. He tests me like this sometimes, to see what I've learned.

"It's haunting. You can only see part of the person and the helmet. It's like the photographer is making a statement about what's not there instead of what is. And maybe the photographer is a little scared to show reality, like it's too horrific to really look at what happened to that soldier. Does that make sense?"

George's face creaks into a smile. "You have good instincts, Soph. Let's look at this one."

He passes me another photo, and we fall into a comfortable rhythm. He points out the things I miss about composition and focus and lighting.

I hang on to his words, wrapping my mind around the lesson and my heart around a moment of kindness from a man who is not my father.

Six months ago, my father didn't yell when he had to pick me up from the principal's office at the end of my first day of school. Somehow the principal had reached him, and my father had returned early from his fishing trip. Principal Barkley had calmly explained why I had been kicked off the cheerleading squad and why he was considering suspending me. My father, equally as calm, explained why Barkley had better reconsider his position on suspension, seeing as how he'd also have to suspend every student who had illegally texted or e-mailed a compromising photo of a minor. A Mexican standoff occurred, and my father never blinked.

An hour later I followed my father out of the school—not suspended but taking the rest of the day off at my father's request.

"Follow me home," he said, unable to look at me. "We'll talk when we get there."

For a heartbeat, I'd hoped he would hear me out. But the way he gripped the folder he'd taken from Barkley, crumpling the edges and most likely the picture of me within, I knew I couldn't count on him.

Three hours later, after alternately yelling at me for shaming our family (i.e., damaging his reputation) and freezing me out, he drove me to the VA Hospital without explanation. He introduced me to Jerry Bausch, their program specialist, with a few terse words.

"Jerry, I thought you might need some help on the Veterans History Project. Quinn is going to be volunteering here after school three days a week until she graduates. I'll be back to pick her up at 1730 hours."

My head shot up. That was news to me.

My father shook hands with Bausch and walked away, not sparing another glance toward me. Perhaps I looked like I would cry, because Bausch acted very kind, while he explained what I would be doing.

In an effort to help people understand the experiences of veterans and war, the hospital participated in the Veterans History Project. My job would be to collect photos, letters, diaries, and other documents from any veterans who wanted to take part.

"We also interview the vets," Jerry said as I tripped down the hall after him. "But you don't have to worry about that. George—one of our long-term patients—handles the interviews, although he may want your help entering it all into a computer."

Jerry tapped on the door to room 222B and entered without waiting for a response. The stark hospital room sat empty. Jerry poked his head back out into the hall and called out to a passing nurse, "Any idea where George is?"

The nurse went from irritated to smiling at the mention of George's name. "Try the west entrance. He said something about taking some pictures outside."

"Right, thanks," Jerry said, as if he should have known.

Feeling very much like a puppy on a leash, I trailed after him down to the lobby, out the west entrance, and across the parking lot to the edge of property where an old man in a wheelchair fiddled with a camera. He was missing a leg, his pants leg conspicuously folded at the knee.

"Hey, George! I want you to meet someone."

The man glanced up, scowled at Jerry, and I thought, *Awesome. I get to hang with a grouchy old geezer three days a week for the next nine months.*

"This is Lieutenant Colonel Quinn's daughter." Jerry announced this with an air of importance, as if George would care who my father was. George spat on the ground, making it clear he didn't give a shit, and I started liking him a little more.

Jerry tried again. "She's going to be helping you with the Veterans History Project." He shifted uncomfortably when the man said nothing, merely stared at him. "Well, then. I'll go ahead and leave you to it."

Jerry nodded at me and practically ran back to the hospital, abandoning me with Groucho. *Asshole.*

"Asshole."

Surprised at hearing my thought echoed out loud, I glanced at George and found him peering at me.

"You're not one of those self-entitled kids who acts like a snotty bitch, are you?" he asked in a gruff voice.

I'd been through the wringer that day and didn't feel like putting up with some stranger's crap, so I said the first thing that came into my head.

"You're not one of those cranky old people who uses their age as an excuse to be a prick, are you?"

We stared each other down. A siren sounded in the distance. A bird chirped from a nearby tree. And then George started laughing. The choking sound made me want to slap him on the back to dislodge whatever had gone down his windpipe.

"Smart-ass," he said without heat. "Get over here. There's a shot I want to get, and I can't do it from this damned chair."

I edged closer, and he shoved his digital camera toward me. On autopilot, I gripped the camera with my right hand, placing my index finger on the shutter button. My left hand cradled the lens.

George gave me an approving nod. "You know how to hold a camera."

I shrugged. The camera Uncle Eddy had given me had broken long ago, and my father had never replaced it. While I'd had it, I'd loved taking pictures, though. Loved seeing how I could freeze time.

"But do you know how to use it?" George challenged.

I shook my head, and he proceeded to spend the hour giving me my first photography lesson. Somehow he managed to be surly and patient at the same time.

We stopped when the sun disappeared behind the clouds. I handed the camera back to George and moved behind him to push his chair.

"I can do it!" he said sharply, hitting the brake.

I knocked his hand away. Having dealt with macho men my entire life, I knew all about hurt pride. "And drop your camera? I just found a reason to like you. Don't take it away so soon."

He huffed a breath that sounded like a half-chuckle. "You're kind of a brat, aren't you?"

I found myself surprised to be smiling on what felt like the worst day of my life, and all because of this grouchy old man. Maybe my punishment wouldn't be so bad.

"What the hell is your name, girl? It's rude not to introduce yourself."

"Oh, like you know all about having manners." Another huff and I grinned at the back of his gray head. I stopped at the entrance to the elevator and walked around the chair to face him. "I'm Sophie Quinn."

We shook hands.

"Sophie, I think you and I will do just fine."

Nobody called me Sophie. Not since my mom had left. But I didn't correct him.

"If you hit on me, I'm out of here," I said, my hand still in his. "That's just creepy."

"Oh, please. You're barely out of diapers." George loosened his grip and rolled his chair onto the elevator. He called over his shoulder, "Nice to meet you, brat."

"Thanks for the lesson," I yelled.

He waved a hand over his shoulder and disappeared when the elevator doors closed.

"Hey, George?"

"Hmm," he answers absently. He is still poring through Don's photos.

"I have to go. It's almost dinnertime."

"'Kay. Night, Soph." He looks up when I am shoving my arms into my jacket sleeves, his gray eyes sharp. "I know the snow is gone, but the roads are still icy. You drive carefully, you hear me?"

It feels so nice so have someone worry about me. Before he can react, I drop a kiss on his forehead. "I promise. See you soon."

"Not if I see you first, brat."

Laughing, I walk out of the room, leaving behind the candy and the Cubans.

I bypass the stairs and regret it when I enter an elevator going up. A doctor exits onto the third floor. I impatiently hit the button for the lobby. The elevator doors are closing when a nurse rolls a sleeping man on a gurney down the hall, and I recognize him.

Corporal Edward Topper. Uncle Eddy.

Chapter Ten

The mirrored elevator door reflects my shocked face back at me.

Mouth open, eyebrows raised, glazed eyes wide.

I am frozen until the doors open on the first floor and a doctor gets on the elevator. He pauses for a moment when I stand there, unmoving, his expression wavering between concern and irritation, like he thinks I'm going to break down in the elevator. That finally gets my feet moving. I make it as far as the straight-backed chairs in the lobby before I collapse, dropping my bag at my feet.

Uncle Eddy.

How long has it been? Five years? No, six. Six years since he drove away with my mother in the passenger seat of his cherry Buick. Six years of wishing and wondering, my thoughts wandering from *Maybe they can't call because they moved to some remote town in Africa to become missionaries* to *Are they dead, their bones rotting in some lost graveyard like Josephine, Thomas, and Susie?* Six years of junior high, high school, best friends, lost friends, and my missing boyfriend. Six years of living with my father and his rules and his expectations and his *Dinner at 1800, you do what I say, you're Quinn now not Sophie.* Six long years and he shows up out of the blue in the VA Hospital down the road from my house.

Uncle Eddy.

A red filter colors my vision.

I hate him. I want to rip his eyes out of his head and shove them down his throat. I want to roll him out of the hospital, push him off that gurney, and leave him to die in the freezing cold.

I bite my lip until it bleeds, and the iron tastes like molten rage. He stole my mother. I needed her more than he *ever* could, and he took her.

And as I sit there in that stupid, uncomfortable lobby chair, the elevator doors open again and my mother exits. She appears, strolling toward me like she'd never left. My mind clicks into a fast shutter speed, snapping continuous frames of her.

Her black hair is longer and pulled back. Elegant. Her lips are no longer berry-stained, but she is Elizabeth Taylor. Except she is no longer the Elizabeth Taylor of *Cat on a Hot Tin Roof.* She is older, I realize. Thirty-eight on her most recent birthday.

Her walk is different too. She no longer glides, her hips swaying in a sensual figure eight. Gravity has caught up and tugged her to the ground. Even her eyes pull down at the corners as she glances toward me with a hint of a frown.

Uncle Eddy must have seen me in the hospital at some point. He's told her I'm here, and she's come to the lobby in search of me. She draws closer and I am shaking, my heart banging against my ribs like it could leap out at her if only my body would let it.

Ten feet, eight feet, six feet.

She almost reaches me, and my stomach clenches in anticipation of a hug, a confrontation, an *I'm so sorry I left you, baby*. I don't know if I should hug her or hate her. Hug. Hate. Hug. Hate.

Hug. I flow to my feet. My mouth opens—

And she walks past me.

Her expression does not change, and her step never falters. I stare at the back of her head until she disappears through one of the exits, tugging her black trench coat close to her body.

She saw me. My mother saw me and walked away like I was nothing.

Again.

I break.

It takes forever for me to calm down, for the quiet sobs to stop, for me to relive every second of her walk through the lobby. Over and over, I picture the expression on her face when she glanced at me.

Blank. Polite.

One stranger passing another. She didn't recognize me. My own mother didn't know me from a stranger standing in a hospital lobby.

What do they say? That a mother will know her own child even if they've been separated?

Bullshit.

My reflection appears in the window behind my chair. I feel drained. Not Sophie. Not Quinn. Not Q. Not anybody.

Six years have changed me, too.

I am hollow.

No eleven-year-old should have to choose between her parents.

After I found Uncle Eddy in my parents' bed, things changed between my mother and me. The months my father spent in Iraq had anchored me to my mother. She was my ballast—sturdy, strong, balancing the upheaval my father's absences and reentries blew into our lives.

"You're too young to understand," she said that afternoon in the car as we drove home from Carey's, where she'd found us holding hands on his porch.

I studied the view out the passenger window, wondering what I hadn't understood. Mom. Uncle Eddy. Naked in my parents' bed. I was eleven, not stupid.

She kept talking. "I love your daddy, Sophie. You know that."

She pulled the car into our driveway, and I turned to see her gazing at me, pleading. That look confused me.

"Are you and Uncle Eddy getting married?" I asked.

She recoiled, her eyes round with surprise. It took her two tries to speak. "No! Geez, Sophie, no!"

"Are you and Daddy getting a divorce?" I bit the inside of my cheek so I wouldn't cry again.

That time she didn't answer so quickly. Her hands gripped the steering wheel until her knuckles turned white. Her lips—bare of any lipstick for once—tightened at the corners in a tense frown. Finally she said, "I don't know, baby. I'm not sure we can all keep on like this."

Her blue eyes blurred with tears, but she no longer seemed bitter. She looked sad. And scared. I'd never seen her afraid. I threw myself against her.

Her arms closed around me, and her sigh lifted my head against her chest. "Oh, Soph."

"I won't tell, Mommy. I promise."

I didn't know I was lying, but I think she did. She held me anyway.

For the next two weeks we continued living our lives like always. During the hot days, I played with Carey and Blake, returning home dirty and exhausted. Uncle Eddy disappeared, or at least he never showed up when I was around. And my mother . . .

She sat on the porch swing, pushing off the ground with a bare foot, her eyes latched on to something in the distance that I couldn't see. During dinner I would be telling her about my day, but she was no longer part of my world. She'd become a ghost I couldn't catch hold of. Worse, she'd made excuses to avoid speaking to my father when he called. Even when they'd fought, she had always spoken to him. Every conversation could be the last. We all knew that. But my mother, she seemed to be slipping away.

I could think of only one person strong enough to make her stay. One person whose word was law in our house. If my father told her to stay, she would do it.

So I broke my promise to my mother.

When my father called home, I told him what I'd seen. He didn't ask to speak with my mother. He didn't comfort me. Instead, he told me to get to bed and hung up.

I went to bed, scared I wore my guilt on my skin. That my mother would come to tuck me in and guess what I'd done. But she didn't come into my room that night, or any other night that week. I started to fear that she would never tuck me in again. She hardly looked at me, but sometimes I would catch her staring at me with great pain, as if she knew I'd betrayed her.

So when she dropped me off at my grandmother's soon after, I knew she was mad at me. She drove away with Uncle Eddy, and I guessed she was leaving my father.

But I never—not once—expected her to leave me, too.

If only I'd just kept my damned mouth shut.

The longer I sit in the shadows of the hospital lobby, the more the rage expands, stretching into corners inside of me. Questions pile on top of one another in incomplete, incoherent, half-formed thoughts. *How could she—? Where have they—? What are they—? Why?*

My muscles tighten with the effort to be still when I feel like I could explode and burn the hospital down with Edward inside it.

Surveillance, I decide.

I will stake out the hospital. Every free minute I have, every minute I am not at school or imprisoned in my room, I will be here, waiting for her to return.

Some screwed-up part of me hoped she'd died in a car accident five minutes after she'd driven away. I fantasized that her last thoughts were of me, wishing she'd never left. The stupid daydreams of a naive little girl.

Because the truth is, she really did abandon me. Like I was scum. Like I was NOTHING. Like she guessed I would become Sophie Topper Quinn, town slut. Unworthy of her, the original town slut.

Too damned bad for her.

I have things to say.

And I don't really give a shit if she wants to hear them.

Chapter Eleven

I don't tell my father I have seen them. I don't even consider it. I'm not sure what he would do, if anything, but there is a slim chance he could make them leave. He has power in our world. I will not allow them to leave before I talk to my mother.

Now I have another secret.

Seven for a secret never to be told.

School sucks, but not like before.

I am different.

The rage, rekindled when my mother nonchalantly walked through the hospital, burns slow and bright. I think my skin glows with it, because the threats and the cruel treatment stop. Badass Jamie pushes me in the hallway once. I spin to face her, and something about me sends her backing away with a new caution. In the week that follows my mother's visit to the hospital, Jamie does not bother me again.

I've waited at the hospital in the evenings as much as I can, but I haven't seen Uncle Eddy or my mother again. I decided not to ask questions. I don't want them knowing I'm looking for them. Now I live for the weekends when I will have uninterrupted hours to search them out.

And then on Friday, my superawesome luck strikes again.

Mr. Horowitz finds me in the library where I've been spending my lunch periods despite Mrs. Hall's harsh stares. I suspect she has tattled on my whereabouts when she tilts her head toward me as if Horowitz has asked her a question. He approaches my table, and I slam my book shut, tipping my head at Mrs. Hall with defiance when she looks down her nose at me. Maybe it wasn't such a great idea to snap a shot of her falling asleep on the job today. The flash woke her up on the wrong side of her desk.

"Mind if I join you?" Horowitz asks, his thick brows raised. They look like two aged caterpillars about to brawl.

I shrug, and he sits across from me at the table. Horowitz isn't so bad, but I don't have him for any classes since he teaches sophomore English. He and his wife are new in town. They moved to Sweethaven last year, when Mrs. Rocher finally retired after forty years.

"You're a chatty one, aren't you?" he says in the silence that follows.

I've been quiet too long, I realize. Months, in fact. It just seems easier to keep secrets when you keep your mouth shut. I shrug again.

He stretches an arm across the chair next to him and studies me. I can't be much to look at these days, armored in flannels, jeans, and boots. The better to hide my body after the picture that revealed too much.

Horowitz's brown hair flops on his forehead. My hair is curly; his is spring-loaded. "That yours?" He points to the Nikon sitting on the tabletop.

I nod. I'm rarely without it these days. I don't trust others not to mess with it if I leave it in my locker. Better yet, you never know when a good picture will come along.

"May I?" he asks. At my nod, he picks up the camera and turns it on. "Nice," he says with a tiny smile. "I think you caught the real her."

The shot of the sleeping Mrs. Hall is on the tiny screen. George hates pictures like this, preferring action shots, but I find something interesting in how unguarded people are when they relax.

Awake, Mrs. Hall is aggressively cheerful, smiling brightly at most everyone. Asleep at her desk, Mrs. Hall's mouth droops into the saddest frown, her head resting on an outstretched arm, reaching for someone who is not there. My guess is, her husband. It's no secret she still grieves for him, though it's been three years since he died in Baghdad.

Horowitz takes his time, flipping through the pictures on the screen. Some he pauses over longer than others. Most of them are of George and Don Baruth from the day before. They'd played poker as George interviewed Don about his Korean War experiences. Don had smiled sweetly and nodded when I'd asked if I could take a few pictures.

"Who's this?" Horowitz asks, showing me a shot of George.

"Someone I work with at the VA Hospital," I say.

"You care about him very much," he says, tapping the camera thoughtfully.

Curious, I lean forward to study the LCD screen. "Why do you say that?"

"He looks upset, angry even, but somehow you managed to show him with compassion."

He's right. George was angry, listening to Don speak about the treatment he'd received at various hospitals when he'd first returned from Korea. Or rather, the lack of treatment he'd received. PTSD—Don said the doctors called it "operational exhaustion" in those days. It hadn't been understood—still isn't fully understood—and it'd caused him to lose his family and his home. He hadn't been able to shut off the violent reactions he had to normal, everyday situations, like how certain noises could set him off. Almost sixty years later, the nightmares haven't stopped, and I wonder if my father has them too. George does. He told Don so in his rough voice when the older man set down his cards and started to cry.

Horowitz shuts off the camera and places it on the table in front of me. "You're very talented, Miss Quinn."

"And?" He must want something from me. Why else would he seek me out in the library?

He laughs. "I'm not very subtle, am I? My wife says it's a fault." He places his hands on the table palms up. "Here's the thing. Yearbook needs a photographer. My kids are doing their best, but it's not really their forte. If I don't get some decent shots in the next two months, we're going to end up with a lot of cut-off heads. You're always hauling that thing around, so I thought maybe . . ."

"You know who I am, right?"

He actually blushes, but his eyes never leave mine. "You can take pictures. That's all I care about."

I have to give him credit for not jumping on the Slay Sophie Quinn bandwagon. But then, he's not from here. It's hard to remember that the rest of the world doesn't live by our code. Maybe Horowitz sees more shades of gray.

"Look, I appreciate the offer, but you have to know it would never work. People don't exactly smile and say 'Cheese' when they see me."

He folds his hands and considers me. He doesn't look ready to give up, and I sigh.

"Seriously, this is a bad idea."

"Think of it as something to put on your college applications."

"I'm a senior," I counter. "That ship sailed last semester." I'd applied to a few schools with photojournalism programs in the fall, but I didn't yet know if I'd been accepted. Boston University was my dream school, but I wasn't holding out any great hope.

"Okay," he says. Now he squares his shoulders like he's getting ready to negotiate. "What can I do to convince you?"

I'm tempted to roll my eyes, but I stop to think about his request. Maybe there is a way to work this to my advantage.

"Sixth period," I say. "I have study hall with Mr. Baransky." And Nikki, who likes to use the class to torture me. "You get me out of sixth period, and I'll take your photos."

"Deal!" He says it so quickly I wonder if that's what he intended all along. I'm sure it is when he continues. "I'll have you transferred into my sixth-period Yearbook class tomorrow. You free tonight for your first assignment?"

I scowl and give a sharp nod. I can't exactly admit I'd rather be stalking the halls at the hospital. He takes a slip of paper out of his back pocket and tosses it down next to my elbow.

Horowitz nods at the paper. "Think candid shots. And welcome to the Yearbook staff, Miss Quinn."

He practically skips out of the room, and I pick up the paper with suspicion. A ticket. *The Spring Semiformal*, I read. The last place I'd want to be tonight, and he knew it.

Ambushed. Damn, Horowitz is good. He'd make a great soldier.

At dinner that night, I tell my father about Horowitz asking me to cover the dance for Yearbook. He grunts and continues eating his meat loaf. I take that as him giving his permission to go.

Standing in front of my closet a half hour later, I curse Horowitz. I have nothing to wear. It's bad enough I'm going, but the best dress I own is the one I wore to last year's spring dance and it's now too big. I hadn't realized I'd lost weight, but it doesn't surprise me, considering I don't eat half the dinner my father serves every night. Our neighbors' brown Labrador, Rueger, has gained ten pounds, though, eating all the steak, meat loaf, and pot roast I've given him. Mr. Daltry swears old Rueger grins like an idiot whenever he sees me from their front window.

I wish I could be at the hospital searching for my mother instead of going to a stupid dance. Thinking of my mother, I remember the few belongings of hers that I'd secreted away in the attic. She'd left some of her clothes and jewelry behind in her hurry to get away from us. My father had thrown out most everything, but I'd managed to hide a few things.

It takes minutes of searching through dusty boxes to find a dress that fits me. Violet chiffon ruffles fall below a ribbon sash at the waist, and a sweetheart neckline hugs me, set off by the two cap sleeves. The dress is perfectly modest, but I feel decadent wearing it. After dressing, I barely have time to throw my hair back into a messy knot and add a tiny headband for decoration. A little makeup and I'm out the door with my camera and my coat.

Walking through the gym entrance, I remember a different time, a better time, when Carey walked in at my side. Graduating early meant Carey missed prom, graduation, and his senior trip. So he'd insisted we make the most of Homecoming. I'd agreed, wanting to hold on to him for as long as I could.

Blake, Angel, and I had laughed our asses off when Carey was crowned Homecoming King to Jamie's Queen. She had campaigned hard, though, and deserved it, but Carey grimaced his way through the ceremony. He dropped his crown on my head as soon as he left the stage, refusing the King and Queen couple's dance. Jamie had glared at me for the rest of the night, but I hadn't cared as Angel and I danced circles around the boys.

Good times. The best times.

Now, any hope I had that I would go unnoticed in the dark gym is lost when I arrive to find Angel and Nikki working the ticket table at the entrance.

Nikki takes one look at me and snaps, "No way. We don't have any tickets left."

I hand my ticket to Angel. "Relax, Nikki. I'm here to work. Yearbook."

Angel takes the ticket. "Since when are you on Yearbook staff?" she asks, curiously.

My smile is wry. "Since Mr. Horowitz conned me into it this afternoon."

She points to my coat. "Let me check that for you."

Something about Angel has changed. She hasn't smiled at me, but she seems nicer than before. It makes me suspicious, but

I unbutton my coat and pass it to her. I hear a whistle, and turn to find Josh Danvers standing behind me.

His appreciative look turns into a scowl. "Oh, it's you."

"Nice to see you too, Josh."

Nikki glares at me, and I remember she's dating Josh this week. "Nice dress," she says, but it's clear she doesn't mean it.

"Thanks," I reply anyway. I don't mention it was my mom's. I'm not stupid enough to bring those comparisons on myself. Instead, I nod at Angel and head into the gym with my camera.

The gym has been transformed into a "Springtime in Paris" theme, with cardboard Eiffel Towers propped against the walls and tissue-paper flowers hanging from the ceiling. Students are having their pictures taken in front of a one-dimensional Arc de Triomphe, and the place has been lit up to resemble the City of Light. It actually looks pretty amazing, though the scent of sweat lingers under all the glitter.

A few people watch me. Feeling out of place, I put my camera to my eye and start snapping pictures. It takes a while, but as I move about the room, I lose myself, focused on capturing the perfect shot of Emmy Hawn dancing with Charles Brown. They look so in love, so unaware of anything outside their bubble, and I hope, for their sake, they can stay there.

Then Sam Ivanov dominates the dance floor when the music speeds up, and people are gathering around him to watch. These shots will show their faces shining with laughter and their bodies completely relaxed, swaying to the music.

Before I know it, an entire hour has passed. I finally manage a break and grab myself some juice. I sit at an empty table and take a sip, making a face at the alcohol aftertaste. Josh Danvers must have struck again with the flask he'd swiped from his father. Carey and I used to laugh about this, picturing Josh as a frat boy at whatever party school he ended up at.

Josh is a jerk, but I kind of miss him. Which is entirely pathetic because I'd never liked him all that much. The idiot used to put his hand on my leg when Carey wasn't around.

As if thinking about him can make him materialize, he appears beside me. He's wearing his usual belligerent look, and I grimace.

"Hey, Josh," I say, praying he's not here to pick a fight.

"Hey, Q. You think Carey knows you're here partying while he's off getting tortured?"

Nice. Right for the throat. I'm tempted to ask him why it's okay for him to party. He's Carey's friend, after all. But the double standard is alive and well in our town, and I don't want to fight. I gather my camera and rise, intending to leave. He blocks my path, and I close my eyes, feeling like I'm living out a stupid teen movie cliché. I try to step around him, and he heads me off again, bringing the scent of whiskey with him. He's either drunk or on his way to it.

"Look, I just want to leave, okay?" I say in a quiet voice.

"No, it's not okay. Nothing you've done is okay. I can't believe you stabbed him in the back the way you did. He was my friend."

"Is."

"What?" Josh asks, confused.

"Carey *is* your friend." It's a stupid thing to point out, but I can't let it go. "Don't talk about him like he's dead."

"Suddenly you give a shit about him?" He's towering over me, and I'm scared as hell because Josh is not my friend, but somebody who is big and muscled and pissed off. I try to leave again, and he grabs my arm. He's not hurting me, but I'm looking around for someone to help me and worrying that no one will because they all hate me and—

And that's when I see Blake standing behind Josh.

Chapter Twelve

Blake places a hand on Josh's shoulder to get his attention. Josh tries to shrug it off without turning to see who is behind him, but he can't shake loose from Blake.

"Hey, man," Blake says in a deep, calm voice. "You mind? I want to dance with Q."

I'm sure I look as shocked as Josh does when he sees Blake.

Josh snorts a half-laugh at Blake. "Right. Very funny."

I use the distraction to slip past both boys. I take a few steps before I am stopped by a hand on my arm. Tired of being grabbed, I yank away. It's Blake's hand, I realize, when the fingers remain gentle.

"Easy," he whispers to me, before giving his attention back to Josh.

"You're serious?" Josh says to Blake.

I glance around. The buzz of laughter and conversation have

hushed. The music plays, but everyone has stopped dancing. For once, all eyes are on Blake and Josh instead of me.

Blake shrugs. "I'm getting tired of everyone acting shitty toward Q. I don't think Carey would put up with it if he were here. You and I both know how he feels about her. It stops now."

There is some kind of warning passing between them that I don't understand. Josh doesn't exactly back down, but Blake walks away as if the conversation is over. He tugs me along with him, and I follow in shock. I feel sick, my body moving sluggishly, overloaded by pent-up fear. We reach the middle of the dance floor, and a slow song comes on. Blake shoulders my camera, takes my right hand in his left, and places his right hand on my waist.

"Put your hand on my arm," he says near my ear. "We're just dancing."

We danced once before, but it turned into more than "just dancing." That's how we got here. I hesitate, but with all eyes on us, I feel like I can't refuse without making a bigger ass of myself. I put a tentative hand on his shoulder and follow his lead as we sway to the music. I try to look anywhere but at him. Instead, all I see is him.

Blake's not wearing a suit like the other boys. He's disheveled and wrinkled in jeans and a gray T-shirt with a faded AC/DC logo. Probably his brother's. He'd thrown a suit coat on over the shirt, but it's obvious he hadn't intended to come to the dance.

"You look beautiful, Q."

I finally let my eyes meet his solemn gaze. I'm so uncomfortable, my skin wants to crawl away.

"What are you doing here?" I ask, and the anger that began when I saw my mother snaps in my voice. He doesn't seem to hear it.

"Angel called," he explains. "She heard Josh getting riled up after he saw you arrive and thought you might need help. The better question is, what are you doing here?"

"Yearbook. And you didn't really answer *my* question. Why did you come here to help me?"

By confronting Josh and dancing with me, Blake's making it clear that nobody should mess with me. I'm confused. He's let me bear the fallout all these months. Why come to my defense now?

Blake is silent so long I think he's not going to answer when he says, "I don't know. Angel called and I had this picture of Carey in my head, screaming at me to get my ass down here. No matter what we've done, he wouldn't want anyone to hurt you."

It sounds so perfect. He's defending me because Carey would want him to. It's not about me. It never is, with these two boys. Blake lets me take the blame, and Carey uses me.

I'm bruised from the inside out. And so damned tired of keeping my mouth shut. I'm beyond tempted to tell the truth. I can see their faces now. *Hey, everyone. You know how you're punishing me because I cheated on that guy? He's freaking gay and made me promise not to tell any of you. Oh, and by the way, the guy I DIDN'T cheat with? He's Carey's bestie, and he let you all believe that he's a damned saint.*

Screw them all. To hell with Carey. And to hell with Blake.

I stop dancing. "So you're a hero? The big, strong guy saving the helpless girl?"

He stops swaying too. "I would never call you helpless."

He blames me for convincing him to betray Carey, but I don't care anymore. The hell I've been through this year has to make up for what I did to him. I never pointed the finger at him. That has to count for more than he's due.

"Should I kiss the ground you walk on because you finally stood up for me?"

"Stop it, Q," he says softly. "I don't expect anything."

"No? What did you say to me before? *'Tell them, Q,'*" I say, mimicking his voice, and he looks ashamed.

I start to tell him how he's misjudged me. How they all have.

And then I picture Carey's face when he begged me to keep his secret last August. And I imagine his parents' shattered faces when they find out what their son was too afraid to tell them. What if they learn that Carey didn't trust them with the truth?

I come to the same conclusion I have a thousand times. It's not my secret to tell. I made a promise and, whether he deserves my loyalty or not, I'll keep it. Because I won't be that person who goes back on her word. Never again.

But despite my silence, I won't let them walk all over me anymore.

"Stay away from me," I say in a hollow voice.

"Q?" Blake sounds upset.

I just want to get away from him. He reaches for my hand. Stiff and unyielding, I freeze him out until he gives up. It's easier to be strong when I'm cold inside. My father has that right, at least.

"I don't need your help, Blake," I tell him. "I've survived all this time without you or Carey. I don't need either of you. Not anymore."

From the way his hazel eyes narrow, I know I've wounded him. Blake passes me my camera when I reach for it, and he doesn't stop me when I walk away.

I give Angel a curt nod of thanks when she gives me my coat. She didn't have to call Blake, and it was nice to know she'd stopped being mad at me long enough to be worried about what Josh might do.

Horowitz, on the other hand, will probably be upset that I didn't stay to see the crowning of the dance's king and queen. Oh well. He'd tricked me into coming here, so he'd better be happy with the pictures I did take. They're all lucky I didn't ruin their idiotic dance by screaming my head off when Josh cornered me.

This honor crap isn't for the weak.

Dad has left the porch light on for me.

It takes all of ten minutes to hide my mother's dress in the back of my closet and get ready for bed. I head to the kitchen in my robe and slippers and make myself a bowl of cereal, eating by the light of the stove. Standing at the counter, I munch away and sort through the mail I'd dropped there earlier. Since the college brochures started pouring in last year, Dad has left it to me to toss away the junk and leave the real mail on his desk.

My fingers pause on the envelope with the words FREE MAIL written where a stamp would go. Only deployed soldiers can send mail that way. It's addressed to me. From Carey.

He's alive, he's alive, he's alive. He's writing to tell me he's okay. I sink to the floor with my back against the counter, shredding the envelope as I go.

No.

The letter is dated. He wrote it weeks ago, before he went missing. Probably when I refused to answer his e-mails. I start crying as I read.

Dear Quinn:

God, you don't know how much I miss you. I think about you all the time, and I imagine us sitting on your porch. Whenever I'm scared or too tired to keep moving, I go there to that porch with you. Your feet are dirty from going barefoot all day, and your hair is tangled and you look more beautiful than you think you are. We're arguing about who is smarter—women or men—and I can tell you think you've won the argument because you're wearing that smug look you get when you think you're right, which is pretty much all the time.

I'd give my left arm to be there with you now. But then I'd want to be back here with my brothers. We're doing a good thing.

I believe that most days. I have to, or I wouldn't be able to make it through. MREs, the freezing nights, the bugs. And those aren't the worst things.

Quinn, I saw my battle buddy get killed today. One minute he was standing next to me, talking my ear off. The next, a sniper got off a shot and I was covered in my buddy's brains and blood. He was talking about his wife's cooking, and then he was just dead. And the only thing I could think about was how sorry I was that I'd left you holding the bag back there. You and Blake.

I know you're angry, and I don't blame you. I should've been a better man. I will be, if I get the chance to come home. I know I don't deserve it, but I need another favor.

Keep my secret a little longer. I'm going to call home as soon as I can get my hands on a phone. I'm going to tell my parents the truth. I owe it to them and to you. Give everyone my love, and give my mom a hug for me. Please write back. I need to know you're okay.

Love,

Me

I drop my forehead to my knees and try to smother the sobs so my father won't hear them. I've been so pissed at Carey, punishing him with my silence. The Carey who wrote this letter? *This* is my Carey—not the one who kept quiet while I took the blame for something I didn't do. It's been so long since I've seen this Carey, the one who taught me what honor and friendship are about.

Missing Carey is boring a hole in me. What if I never see him again?

Last summer, after Carey told me he was gay, I felt like my entire world had splintered. And I hated him for doing that to me. After crying for two hours, I picked myself up, put on some makeup to cover the mess I'd made, and dressed in my sexiest tank top and jeans.

I'd come to the conclusion that something was wrong with me. It had never even occurred to me that Carey didn't want me in that way. Who the hell dates a gay guy and doesn't notice? A stupid girl, I'd guessed. Still . . . Why hadn't I pushed him? Why had I accepted our passionless relationship? Because, if I was being honest with myself, I hadn't wanted to push him. I liked how comfortable we were. What did that say about me? In trying not to be my mother, had I completely turned off my feelings and become my father? Become a prude instead of a whore?

I left my house that summer night with something to prove. I pretended I wasn't sure where I was going or who I was going to. What a lie.

Blake and me, we'd always had a rocky friendship. Carey had brought us together whether we liked it or not, and we'd accepted each other for him. But Blake had an edge when he watched me with Carey. Something dark sparked in his eyes when we found ourselves alone. Over the summer, with Carey away at Camp Geiger, Blake and I were frequently alone together. Blake had never said a word—would never betray Carey that way—but some part of me suspected what it was that he was holding back.

That night, I wanted to hear those things Blake wouldn't bring himself to say. I needed to hear them.

I didn't feel nervous until I stood on his porch.

I took a deep breath to find the courage—or stupidity—that had brought me there.

Blake opened the door.

Chapter Thirteen

When I knocked on his door, I knew Blake was alone, that his brother worked Saturday nights and his mother was out of town visiting his aunt. Blake answered the door and leaned against the doorjamb lazily.

Clearly I'd woken him up. He wore only a pair of jeans, riding low on his hips, and no shirt. My heart beat a little faster.

He yawned. "Q? Whatdya doing here? Where's Carey?" Blake looked around me as if he expected him to appear.

"We broke up," I said. Three words I thought might change everything.

And they did.

Blake lost all appearance of sleepiness, letting go of the door to stand up straight. I will never forget the look in his eyes at that moment. A hint of danger. And hope.

"Can I come in?"

He started and stepped back in a hurry. "Of course."

I'd been to Blake's house a thousand times since we were kids building forts in the backyard. This time was different. I should have left right then. Instead, I walked past him and into the living room, where I'd once lounged with Carey on the couch, so sure he'd love me forever. Neither Blake nor I sat down now. We stood in the middle of the room, staring at each other awkwardly.

"What happened?" he asked finally.

I shifted, studying the pictures on his mantle so I wouldn't stare at his chest. "He broke up with me."

Blake looked shocked when I turned to face him. "*He* broke up with you?"

I gave a harsh laugh. "Yep. You sound surprised."

He stuck his hands into the back pockets of his jeans. "I am. You guys are Marine Barbie and Ken."

That last bit sounded bitter, echoing what Angel'd always called us. I took a step toward him.

"Did he say why?"

Because he's gay.

I'd thought I was over crying, but the concern in Blake's voice had my eyes filling. I examined the floor, trying to get my emotions under control.

"Shit. I'm sorry. Don't cry."

His arms surrounded me, and I let myself lean into him, breathing him in. Blake had put his arm around me before, laughing while we walked with Carey, but it had never felt like that. *I'd* never felt like that.

"Did he cheat on you, Q? Because I'll kick his ass if you want me to."

His low voice vibrated next to my ear. Heat, I realized. The feeling I'd been missing with Carey was there with Blake. Nerves skittered under my skin wherever he touched me. He rocked me like a person rocks a crying child, but it felt like we danced.

I tilted my head back to look at him, and our eyes met for a long, silent moment.

Then I stood on my tiptoes and reached up, up, up to kiss him.

Blake didn't bend to meet me halfway but leaned back, as if his mind couldn't accept what I was doing. He didn't turn his head, though, when I set my lips on his. The kiss didn't feel comfortable at all. It felt terrifyingly good.

I sighed, and he gasped. Then he stumbled back, holding me at the waist as if to push me away.

"Wait! What the hell, Q?" He pulled back a couple of feet, bumping into the wall. "Fuck. You're Q! You're Q, of Carey and Q. We can't do this!"

I shook my head. "I'm not Carey and Q. Not anymore. I'm just me."

"Right," he said, running his fingers through his hair. "And tomorrow the two of you will make up, and I'll be the asshole who made a move on his best friend's girlfriend."

I shook my head again. "We're not getting back together,

Blake. He has feelings for someone else." *And so do I*, I thought, though I'd been slow to understand that.

"So I'm Rebound Guy?" he asked, anger vibrating through him.

What could I say? I didn't know how to answer, so I said nothing. I swayed toward him, pressing into his resisting hands.

"Who am I kidding?" he asked under his breath. "I'll take whatever you'll give me."

He began to pull me in instead of push me away. His breath was on my face when he paused, a questioning look in his hazel eyes. "You're sure?"

"Yes. . . ."

He kissed me for real.

I fell into him. I didn't love him like I loved Carey, but that was kind of the point, right?

His hand slipped beneath my shirt. My heart jumped into my throat.

My fingers trailed down his chest. His breath sucked in sharply, as if I'd tickled him.

We kissed with our eyes open, really seeing each other.

Giving. Taking. Setting each other on fire. Naked.

The way it was supposed to be.

The way it had never been with Carey.

The next night, Carey asked me to lie for him, to pretend we were still together.

And seeing the bruises on his face, how could I not agree?

I couldn't explain to Blake why I'd suddenly changed my mind, and he couldn't forgive me.

I'd used him to prove I wasn't cold and that a boy could want me as more than a friend. My feelings for him were real, but that didn't alter my intent for going to his house. I'm not proud of myself. Maybe that's another reason why I've never told anyone that Blake is the boy in the picture. Well, that, and he thinks I lied to him about Carey and me breaking up.

But I don't regret a minute of that night.

He was my first.

My only.

The events at the dance and Carey's letter leave me reeling. I've hardly slept, thinking about Blake and Carey. Knowing Carey planned to tell the truth makes it a little easier to bear this lie. If he came out to everyone, people would know I didn't cheat on him. I would be free to tell Blake that I felt something for him that night and that Carey didn't care when that picture surfaced.

Carey obviously didn't know how bad things were if he thought I was on speaking terms with his parents. That makes me feel better. I guess his parents haven't said much about me during their calls or in their e-mails. I feel like I should tell them about the letter, since it was his last contact before he went missing. But how?

Too tired for a confrontation, I wait until my father has left the house to run Saturday-morning errands before I leave my room.

George expects me today, so I head to the hospital.

The light hurts my eyes. Everything hurts. I feel like one big, exposed, gaping wound.

I'm heading through the lobby to George's room when Darlene calls my name from the front desk.

"Sophie! George said to tell you he's out having a test done. He'll be back soon if you want to wait."

"Thanks, Darlene."

I stride toward the stairs to wait for George in his room. It seems like lately he's out for more and more tests.

"Sophie?"

The trembling voice is familiar, and I turn to see who called my name.

Uncle Eddy stares at me. "Sophie Quinn, is that you?"

Chapter Fourteen

Uncle Eddy is five years younger than my father, but he's not aging well. The years have softened him. His muscles have dissipated, leaving behind skin and bones. He is too skinny, and what's left of his blond hair has begun to gray. It takes all of two seconds to understand that he is very sick. Maybe dying. I've seen too many men at the hospital look the same way.

"Sophie Quinn?" he asks again, coming closer.

I nod, unable to speak.

"I knew it! I heard that woman call you, and you're the spitting image of your mother with all that hair." Uncle Eddy reaches me and pulls me into a hug. My arms remain locked to my sides, and his hug transforms into an awkward pat on the back as he realizes it is unwelcome.

The whites of his eyes are yellow, I notice, when I pull away.

Kidneys are shot, then. Corporal Lewis in room 308 has been on dialysis for a year, so I know the signs.

"You're all grown up now, aren't you?"

Six years'll do that.

"I saw you," I blurt out. "And my mom."

See what happens when you open your mouth? You say things you meant to hold tight.

"Here at the hospital?"

I nod again.

"You mind if we sit? It's hard for me to be on my feet too long."

He's breathing heavily as I follow him to a corner of the lobby. We sit a couple of seats away from where my mother walked past me a few weeks ago without recognizing me.

Uncle Eddy pauses, trying to catch his breath. After a minute he says, "Forgive me, Sophie."

I know he means for taking a moment to rest, but I say, "For what? Stealing my mom?"

Geez, I sound so hateful, I hardly recognize my voice. Worse, his skin fades to a sickly gray shade, and his eyes close. I'm worried I've shocked him into having a stroke.

I wait for his eyes to open—wintergreen like my father's—and I can see he's okay before I rise. It was childish to think I could tell off him and my mom. Like it would make things better and make the past just go *poof*! As if. Then maybe we could all go back to our house for a family reunion and sweet tea on the porch. Just brilliant.

She left. What difference does it make that she's back?

"I'm going to go—"

"Your mother wants to see you, Sophie."

"Don't call me that." My words surprise us both.

"Sophie?" he asks. "What do you want me to call you?"

SophieTopperQuinnQ. For every name I have, there is someone who objects to it. I don't even know what to call myself.

"Nothing. I don't want you to call me anything."

"O-kay . . ." He draws the word into two syllables, and I can
tell he's thinking I'm some screwed-up teenager hiding a drug
addiction and hefting an attitude through a "difficult phase."

Whatever. I sigh. "Someone's waiting on me. I've got to go."

"Wait! What should I tell your mom?"

His raised voice draws attention. Darlene watches from the
front desk. A nurse from Don's floor glances at us as she passes.
People don't need another reason to gossip about me.

"That's up to you. Honestly, if she wants to see me, I'm sure
she can figure out how to work a phone. If I remember right, she
was a tramp, not stupid."

For a moment, Uncle Eddy looks like he wants to slap me.
I'm almost daring him to, so I can hit back, him being sick or
not. I blame him. And her. Everything shitty about my life
began the day they left.

Uncle Eddy's lips narrow with righteous indignation.

Anger hums in his voice when he speaks, but the words
come slowly, as if he's a drill sergeant lashing a plebe. "You have

a right to be mad, so I'll let that go. Once. Your mom will be waiting for you at the Blue Dawn Café in Spring Lake tomorrow at oh-nine-hundred. Got that?"

I won't feel guilty. Not because of this man. No way will I let him boss me around. My father is bad enough. I toss my bag over my shoulder, throwing as much disdain as I can into the look that I give him.

I shrug. "Doesn't matter. I won't be there."

"Oh-nine-hundred!" he calls after me, but I'm gone, striding past Darlene and slamming through the door to the stairwell.

The better to hide until the trembling stops and I know I won't lose it.

I'm too angry to stay at the hospital.

George doesn't deserve to have me take my temper out on him, so I leave him a note in his room, telling him I don't feel well. Then I drive out to Grave Woods, where some snow lingers, though most of it has seeped into the ground and disappeared. Any day now, my father will have his garden.

I have the camera, but I don't take any pictures. Instead, when I arrive at the graves I lie on the ground, flat on my back between Josephine and Thomas, and stare up at an icicle hanging from a branch overhead. The ice sweats languid drops that trickle to the tip of the ice-stick where they dangle, suspended for *one* . . . *two* . . . *three* seconds before gravity takes over. I study each new drop, predicting how long it can delay the inevitable free fall.

One . . . two . . . three . . .

One . . . two—

I am bits of who everyone thinks I am. *One . . .* Blake's Q. *Two . . .* Carey's Quinn. *Three . . .* Sophie Jr., taking after her whore mom. *Four . . .* middle name Topper for Uncle Eddy the Honorable. Which piece is really me?

I'm plummeting and terrified of hitting rock bottom.

I want to be someone new.

Sophie Topper Quinn, no more.

I wake up because I'm shivering so hard, my bones might shatter.

Day has faded into evening, which means I've been in the woods for hours. A glance at my watch and I know Dad is going to freak because I've missed dinner. Panic drives me to my feet, but it takes forever to get back to the Jeep when I get lost in the dark.

I'm two hours late when I pull in to the driveway. It won't matter that I'm always on time. People never see how good you are. Fuck up once, though, and it's like you are wearing a neon sign.

My father's heard my car. He marches out onto the porch, and he's Lieutenant Colonel Cole Quinn marching on the enemy.

"Damn it, Quinn! Where the hell have you been?"

The heat from the car hasn't thawed me. I'm hugging myself to get warm and my teeth chatter when I try to answer. "I—"

He waves his hand, brushing away my excuses. "I don't

want to hear it! You get your ass into the house. You're the most damned irresponsible . . . I've had it with you, kid."

He leaves me standing in the driveway with my mouth open. The door bangs shut behind him, and I can hear him crashing through the house, slamming doors as he goes. Yelling about what a fuck-up I am. How sad for him to get saddled with a daughter like me.

The unfairness of it slaps me in the face.

I don't think.

Every person has a limit.

There is a small shed set off to the side of the garden. It's where my father keeps his gardening supplies. Funny how the green weed killer and plant-food bottles look so similar. It's easy enough to swap the contents.

My father's so religious about feeding his plants, loving them and hovering over them every day. If I add up every minute he's spent in this garden over the past six years, I know it will out-weigh the time he's spent with me.

I hope the garden stays barren.

"Quinn, wake up. Shh . . . You're okay."

My father shakes me and I'm awake all at once, startled to find him sitting on the edge of my bed with his hand on my shoulder.

"There you are," he says as my eyes focus on him. He drags his work-roughened fingers under my eyes, wiping away tears I didn't know I was crying.

I am six parts ocean.

My father's presence confuses me after our silent warfare. "Dad?" I stop because my throat feels raw.

"You were screaming Carey's name," he explains. "Must've been one helluva nightmare, too," he adds gruffly. "I think you even woke Rueger."

We listen to the Lab barking from next door.

I remember the dream now. I'd been watching the news. A reporter had come on to announce the execution of a prisoner-of-war. The shot had switched to a home video of masked men with swords. Carey knelt before them, and I'd watched as one man cut off his head, holding it up to the camera in triumph. Even now, I shudder reliving it, knowing it could actually happen. Has happened.

"What if he doesn't come back?" I sound like I did when I was a little kid, asking when my mom would come home.

My father hooks my hair behind my ear, like he used to when I was younger and had bad dreams, and I remember how he once-upon-a-time loved me. I clasp his warm hand between mine to make him stay with me, but he pulls away after a few short seconds.

"He's a good man. Don't you give up on him, okay?"

I nod. The house creaks and knocks around us, and Rueger still barks in the distance.

"I didn't know how upset you were, Quinn," my father says. "I came down hard on you."

Tonight the moon shines through the blinds, too bright to camouflage how tired he is. His eyes are pinched the way they were when he first came home from his tour in Iraq after my mom left, and it was just him and me. He's worried, I guess, wondering what the hell to do with me. Raising a daughter alone isn't the life he wanted.

"Sometimes I forget you're not one of my Marines."

"I'm not that strong, Daddy," I whisper.

One side of his mouth concedes a smile. "It's been a long time since you called me that."

Too long.

"You okay now?" he asks, rising.

I don't want to, but I let go. "Yeah. Sorry I woke you."

He pauses in my doorway. "I'm not. I love you, kid. Get some sleep."

My door closes before I can recover enough to tell him I love him, too.

Chapter Fifteen

My alarm isn't set, but I wake early enough to make it to Spring Lake by 0830.

I avoided seeing my father by sneaking out the front door while he poured himself a cup of coffee in the kitchen. Some Sundays I hang out at the hospital, so I'm guessing he'll think that's where I am. In reality, I'm sitting in my Jeep in front of the Blue Dawn Café, waiting for my mother to show and wondering what the hell I'm doing here.

The Blue Dawn Café is set back from the tree-lined sidewalk. The huge square windows frame the picturesque view of the inside with its vinyl booths and the regulars lined up on stools at the bar. It's a freaking Norman Rockwell painting.

Why Spring Lake? I think. Uncle Eddy is Army. Were they stationed at Fort Bragg—a half hour from Sweethaven—all this time? Or did they move back to North Carolina recently? And why now?

The questions whirl through my mind, but I don't have any answers. She does, though. If I find the courage to walk into the diner, I can find out what I want to know. But will I like what I hear? I've learned that things can always suck worse than they did five minutes ago. Do I really want to rock this boat, with its plugged holes and missing oars?

I haven't made any decisions, but it's too late. She's arrived. The café must have a back entrance, because one minute she's not there and the next she's sliding into a booth in the front window.

My mother.

At the hospital, maybe thirty seconds passed from the moment I saw her to when she'd walked out the door. Now, I take my time to absorb the changes. She hasn't aged as much as I'd thought. Perhaps whatever was wrong with Uncle Eddy made her look strained that night.

She is beautiful, but not sultry like I remembered. I can't put my finger on what's different. The longer black hair and the toned-down makeup, obviously, but something more. Something in her attitude. She is a mystery.

I want to know. Everything.

Six years ago, my mother had promised we would take a trip. A train trip to New York City. Or a car ride to Wilmington. I didn't care where we went. I loved that it would be just her and me.

Of course, after I found my mother in bed with Uncle Eddy, she stopped mentioning the vacation, and our getaway dissolved into mist. I knew the call I'd made to my father had sealed the deal. Uncle Eddy had disappeared from our house, and my father had yet to return home from the Middle East. My mother had scarcely noticed me in days, and I'd spent more time at Carey's than at home. At least at his house, Carey tried to cheer me up. He even went so far as to convince Blake to let me pick the movie—*Mulan*—which they both hated and I loved. We did not agree on what constituted a "chick flick."

One night, I'd heard my parents arguing by phone, the words indistinguishable except for my mother screaming "Don't talk to me like I'm one of your fucking Marines, Cole!" and "I married *you*, not the damned Marines." The last she punctuated with a loud, repeated slamming noise.

The next morning at breakfast, I alternated between worried glances at our broken phone, which lay like shrapnel on our kitchen table, and her. Distracted, she exhaled through pursed red lips and stared into the curlicue of smoke drifting above her head.

I shoved my Cookie Crisp cereal in circles around my bowl, dunking them in the milk and watching them bob back to the surface. Unsinkable cookies. Funny how the chocolate chips always looked bigger on the box than in real life.

"Stop playing with your food, Soph," my mother said.

I looked up quickly to find her smashing a cigarette into the fancy white candy dish she used as an ashtray.

Her blue eyes met mine, suddenly fierce. "Let's go some-where."

"Like to the movies?"

She shook her head. "Not the movies. Listen, we can do anything. Where would you want to go right now if you could go anywhere?"

The expectant look on her face weighed on me. She wanted me to pick somewhere exciting. If I said what I wanted—to spend time with her—it wouldn't be the right answer. I shrugged and drank the last of the milk in my bowl.

"You're too much like your father." She sighed and rose to her feet, clearing away my cereal and her ashtray. "You don't always have to be so perfect, Sophie. Be spontaneous."

I grasped enough of that to know I'd disappointed her. "The beach," I blurted out.

"The beach?" she asked as if the idea intrigued her. "I like it," she added decisively, dropping our dishes in the sink with a clatter. "Go pack an overnight bag."

She didn't have to tell me twice. We both rushed through the house, laughing and calling to each other from our rooms. She made it into a race, giving me ten minutes to gather my things and get into our car. I made it in nine and a half.

We didn't stray far from home.

The four hours to Nag's Head on the Outer Banks reas-sured me like my call to my father hadn't. We played games— "Find an object that starts with each letter of the alphabet" and

"I Spy"—and sang along to the radio. When we arrived, my mom splurged on one of those motels that sat right on the beach *and* had a pool.

A few moments of those two days pop out like Polaroids taped to my heart: Savoring saltwater taffy in waxy rainbow shades as we sat in the sand watching the sun color the water. Doing a flip into the pool in my red polka-dot one-piece with the bow on the front while mom clapped from under the shade of a lemon-yellow umbrella. Dancing in our hotel room with the radio turned up loud enough to feel my heart knocking in my chest, and the flash of my mother's skirt as she whipped me around. And at the end of the day, curling up at her feet as her fingers tickled my scalp and she unknotted a day's worth of tangles from my waist-length hair.

For two days she focused every bit of her attention on me. She listened to me chatter on about Carey and Blake. I told her everything I liked and everything I disliked and everything that popped into my head. Unfiltered. Uncensored. Unaware.

And then we returned home to find Uncle Eddy on our doorstep. I snubbed him as only an eleven-year-old can, running past him and stomping into the house. My mother sent me to my room, and their voices rumbled from the kitchen. They did not sound angry, like my parents usually did. They did not argue or shout. No—they spoke in hushed tones, excited whispers. Sharing secrets.

I sat on the floor with my ear to the door, tearing at the skin around my fingernails, but I couldn't make out their words. It didn't matter, though. The next day the two of them picked me up from Carey's house in Uncle Eddy's old Buick. I sat in the backseat with my arms crossed, glaring out the window. I didn't want my mother near *him*. He'd ruined everything.

Instead of driving to our house, we pulled up at my grandmother's. My father's mother, her steel-gray hair coiled into uniform rows of perfect barrel curls, shook her head at my mother. Uncle Eddy used to say that Grandma had sharpened her tongue on my grandfather for so many years, it could flay the skin off a man from one hundred yards away. While my mother and I climbed out of the car, my grandmother approached Uncle Eddy who busied himself pulling a suitcase—my pink suitcase—out of the trunk.

"You've betrayed your brother and this family," she told him, taking the suitcase. "You're not welcome here."

Uncle Eddy's face tightened, like each word had slapped him. "I'm sorry you feel that way, Mom."

She turned to my mother. "And you. You should be ashamed of yourself. I told Cole you would never be a Marine's wife."

My grandmother tried to restrain me, but I shook off her hand. I cinched my arms around my mother's waist.

My mother had never liked my grandmother. She'd spent as little time as possible with her, complaining to my father that Grandma criticized everything from her smoking and her housekeeping to the way she raised me. Despite her feelings, she'd always been polite on our visits, but that mask fell away as we stood there.

"You're right, Ellen," she said. "I'm not cut out for this life."

They exchanged a look that went over my head.

My mother bent to kiss me on the forehead. "Be a good girl, Sophie."

I refused to loosen my grip on her until she whispered in my ear, "I promise I'm coming back."

I felt silly, then, for acting like a baby, clinging to her. My grandmother's hands clamped on my shoulders the second I let my mother go. And we both watched my mother wave good-bye from the passenger's seat of Uncle Eddy's Buick.

What a sad picture I must have made. Sophie Topper Quinn . . . unwanted.

And now she's back. Is she here to keep her promise?

I climb out of the Jeep and walk toward the café. She glances up from a menu when I'm a few feet away from the entrance. This time there is instant recognition when she sees me. Half rising from the booth, she touches the window as if she can reach me through the glass. Emotions flicker across her face, one stampeding into another. Fear. Pain. Need.

I stop and take a step back.

No.

Self-preservation finally kicks in. I can't handle another person needing anything from me. I'll have nothing left if I give another piece of myself away. Why did I come here? She left. She walked away. My father stayed. Every day. Every night I had a nightmare in those weeks after she left. Every dinner was at 1800 hours, whether either of us liked it or not.

She was wrong. When she married my father, she *did* marry the Marines, for better and often for worse. She quit on us.

To hell with her and her needs.

Her mouth forms my name when I climb back into the Jeep. As I reverse out of the parking space, she runs for the café's front door. Then she is a speck in my rearview and I'm regretting my trip to Spring Lake and wondering what this secret is going to cost me.

She broke our family when she broke her promise to return.

And I feel like I've betrayed my father by going there to meet her.

Chapter Sixteen

I'm sitting on a bus with forty-three other seniors and juniors. We outnumber the chaperones eight to one. We're on our way to DC, where we'll tour Capitol Hill, the National Mall, and stare at the White House through the security gates.

Two weeks have passed since I saw my mother in Spring Lake, and little has changed except that my father seems to notice me now from time to time. I almost feel guilty that his garden remains a brown wasteland, but no way in hell am I going to admit what I did. I haven't bumped into my mother or Uncle Eddy again, and I'm glad. What would I say?

For now, I'm lucky Mr. Horowitz chose to take the seat next to me. At least I was able to get some sleep during the long drive. Lately the nightmares won't go away. I trace a drop of condensation on the window. *Come home, Carey.*

"How's your friend?"

I turn to Mr. Horowitz, wondering if he can read minds.

He adds, "The one in the pictures on your camera."

George, then, not Carey.

George is coughing more these days, but he says not to worry. They haven't figured out the right combination of medications to give him. He's like a kid's chemistry set, and the doctors keep mixing things up to see what kind of reaction they can set off.

I shrug, not wanting to get into it. "He's okay."

"Good, good," Horowitz says, nodding cheerfully.

I'm trying to decide if I'm still pissed at him. I never planned to go on this trip, but he conned me into it by feeding my ego. *We need pictures, Miss Quinn. Your work is so beautiful, Miss Quinn, so full of honesty.* He loved the pictures I took at the dance, despite the missing shots of the king and queen. I feel cheap for caving to flattery, but honestly, it's not like a lot of people are nice to me these days. And when George heard about the trip, he asked me for a favor I couldn't refuse.

"I think you mentioned you met him at the VA Hospital?" asks Mr. Horowitz.

His curiosity surprises me, and I'm slow to answer. "Yeah. George does a lot of volunteer work for the Veterans History Project. I help out a few days a week."

Horowitz looks confused, and I explain what the project is. Excited, I turn on my ever-present camera to show him pictures of George, Don, and the others I've met at the VA. I haven't told anyone yet, not even George, but Boston University has accepted me into their photojournalism program. It doesn't seem right to plan my future until I know whether Carey will have one too.

"You wouldn't believe what some of these people have been through," I finish.

He considers me with a new awareness like I've said something he didn't expect. "You sound pretty passionate about working with the military."

It takes a moment for that arrow to plant itself in my chest. I stiffen. "You mean I shouldn't care, after how I treated Carey?"

Horowitz blushes to the matted roots of his curly hair. "I didn't mean it like that," he says, and I think it's true. He's one of those teachers who care about their students. But maybe I'm wrong. Maybe he's heard the gossip about me and judged me for it like the others.

"You don't know me," I say.

The conversation ends when I turn back to the window. Discomfort moves in and takes over the two inches of space between us, but I still prefer this seat to the one beside Jamie.

The bus pulls into the hotel parking lot, and we wait for the driver to unlock the huge undercarriage so we can claim bags. Shivering and shuddering from the cold, I hang back until the crowd disappears into the hotel lobby before I grab my small duffel.

The lobby gleams and shines, despite the loud teens now

loitering about and sprawling on velvet sofas and armchairs. Add a few video-game consoles, TVs, and a soda machine, and we'd make ourselves right at home. Soon the chaperones turn over the distribution of the keys to Jamie and Josh, our trip leaders, and they wander toward the fireplace to warm up while we get sorted out. Jamie and Josh group us together. Two beds in a room, four girls or four guys to a room. Again I hold myself apart, wanting to disappear from this trip where escape into the woods or even my car is impossible.

I needn't have bothered.

Some of the guys, including Blake, wander off, but a lot of the others stick around, even after they have their keys. A sly silence spreads, and looks bounce between Jamie and me. More rooms are assigned and I do the math in my head. There are twenty-one girls: five still await their room keys, including Jamie.

Jamie gives me a smug smile, and I wince. Then she points to Janet Chou. "You can room with me. And you," she adds, pointing to Amery Hoffmeyer.

Danielle Alcala and I are the last ones standing. Of course, Danielle is Jamie's friend. Jamie makes a production of putting the tip of her finger to her lips, playing to her audience. Everyone watches, and my eyes burn with embarrassment.

Finally, she shakes her head, oozing pity. "I don't know, Quinn. I'm not sure I want to share a room with you. I mean, have you had your shots?" She takes a step toward me and drops her voice just enough to go unnoticed by the chaperones. "Who knows what I could catch from bed-jumping trash like you?"

Right. Now my whore cooties can spread through close contact.

I roll my eyes.

Jamie's eyes narrow and she calls out too loudly, "OMG, Mrs. Peringue, we have too many girls! I think Quinn is going to be sleeping in the lobby." She waits for the teacher to join us before adding in her sweetest voice, "Unless someone wants to volunteer to let her sleep on their floor?"

Twenty seconds. That's how long they stare at me, letting me hang.

Finally Angel makes a move to step forward, but Nikki grabs her arm. That's all it takes for Angel to back down, refusing to meet my eyes. Nikki covers her smile with a fist. Clearly enjoying the situation, Josh grins. And the whole time Mrs. Peringue stands there, wringing her hands and doing nothing.

With a little shrug, Jamie says, "Oh well, Quinnie. I tried."

I want to punch her in the face. I hate her. I hate them. I really wish I hated them all.

Mr. Horowitz finally steps in and asks what's going on. He takes charge of the situation. Jamie is on ten, playing teacher's pet. Horowitz listens to her explain how I was a last minute addition and there simply isn't a room for me. I can actually feel myself sinking into the ground, a gelatinous blob of humiliation.

"Well, Jamie, I can see only one solution. Since you're such good friends with these ladies"—he gestures to Nikki and Angel—

"you can take a cot in their room. You won't mind Quinn taking your spot, now will you?"

The last part does not come out like a question. Crossing his arms, Mr. Horowitz waits for her to slap her key in my palm, and then orders us all to our rooms. "Get some sleep, people. We have a busy day tomorrow."

As I pass him, I mutter, "Thanks."

"Anytime," he says.

In the elevator, I shift my duffel to my other shoulder and analyze my feet while people straggle in around me. Someone's feet face mine, and her breath crosses my face, smelling of red hot gum.

"You enjoyed that, didn't you?" Jamie says. Rage boils her low whisper until it blisters my skin. I wish the doors would close already because then I'd be that much closer to getting in a room away from her.

"Nothing to say?" she prods. "No? I guess we all know you're better on your back."

That hurts, but I can deal. It's just more of the same from her.

I ignore her, and she adds, "You're just like your mother. I bet if Carey had a brother you would've slept with him, too."

Bull's-eye. Blake is Carey's brother in all the ways that matter.

Shocked, I hiss a breath and a cold sweat pops up on my skin. Maybe I really am my mother's daughter when it comes to using people. What if everyone figures it out? Figures out Carey's secret? Does she suspect it's Blake in the picture? What will happen to him then? What will happen to Carey's family?

Worse, I can't even defend myself; it's hard to argue with truth.

I tremble and sway on my feet, and Jamie knows she's finally gotten to me. Her eyes glow like light hitting a polished trophy.

The elevator doors begin to slide closed, locking me into this nightmare. Like a coward, I tuck my tail between my legs and shove past the others to slide back into the lobby. I am completely horrified when a sob claws out of my throat.

They hear it. *She* hears it. She laughs, and I bleed.

Last July, my only concerns had been waiting for Carey's leave in August and keeping Nikki out of trouble so she didn't get kicked off the squad for what Coach Breen called "inappropriate behavior." Coach meant the drinking, the boy-chasing, the mean-girl rep, and every other clichéd cheerleader behavior TV had used to label us. Nikki, of course, took the rules as a challenge. For some reason I never understood, she liked to press up to the point of no return without actually crossing over.

One summer day after a grueling practice, we swooped into Angel's house, hot, sweaty, and tired.

I stopped at the mirror in her entryway, staring at the reflection of my neck. "Damn it, Nikki. You gave me another hickey."

Nikki and Angel pressed in close to study the reddish-purple mark Nikki's shoe had left on my neck. Our heads looked interesting together with my black hair, Angel's brunette locks, and Nikki's red mane.

Nikki scowled. "If you had stood still, my foot wouldn't have slipped."

I glared at her, rubbing the mark. "You try not moving with your fat ass standing on my shoulders."

Angel wrapped an arm around our necks, clamping a hand over each of our mouths before we could start arguing for the fifteenth time that day. "I swear, if you two don't cut it out, I'm going to murder you in your sleep tonight. Be nice."

Nikki must have licked Angel's palm because Angel yanked her hand back, wiping it down her side. "Ew! That's disgusting, Nikki!"

She laughed. "You liked it. That's the most action you've had in months. Dibs on the shower!"

Angel and I watched her leave to stake her claim on the bathroom, and Angel shook her head. "I hate it when she's right."

"Luckily, it doesn't happen often."

A couple of hours later, we stared at the remains of the demolished pepperoni pizza and ignored Nikki while she tried to convince us it was a great idea to go blond for the start of school.

"Come on, guys! Show a little backbone. Blondes have more fun! And I want to have hella fun my senior year."

"Not a chance," Angel said. "My mom would kill me."

"Your mom's not here," Nikki grumbled. She instantly smacked a hand over her mouth, her eyes widening when she realized what she'd said. "Oh geez, Ang, I'm sorry. I swear I didn't mean it like that."

Angel's mom had been gone for seven months that tour. A Marine deployed to Iraq, she'd spent more of Angel's teen years overseas than at home, though they e-mailed and talked on the Internet as often as they could.

Angel grimaced and shrugged. "Don't worry about it."

Her father appeared in the living room doorway and eyed the pizza box on the coffee table. It was a graveyard of crusts.

"You didn't leave me any," he accused. "Are you sure you're girls? I swear, you eat like dudes."

"First come, first served," Nikki said, and added, "Where's your sweater, Mr. Rogers?"

With a name like his, Mr. Rogers had long ago grown accustomed to the jokes. "It's with my slippers. I only bring it out for neighbors."

Angel's father doted on her. He even made time for us when we hung out at her house, and he never missed out on the opportunity to cheer her on, no matter how small the achievement. It amazed me how well they got along, and sometimes I wished we could switch families, even though Angel would get the short end of the stick.

Mr. Rogers dropped between us onto the couch, throwing an arm around an embarrassed Angel. "What are we talking about? Boys or other girls?"

Angel elbowed him in the gut. "Parents who don't mind their own business."

Nikki's mobile rang with a dirty song that raised Mr. Rogers's eyebrows. She checked the caller ID and squealed. "It's Josh. Don't wait up."

We watched her go out the sliding glass door to the backyard, answering the phone in a breathy voice as she went.

"Josh?" Mr. Rogers asked.

"Don't ask," Angel muttered.

Her dad focused on me. "Um, Quinn, I hate to tell you this, but you have something on your neck."

I slapped a hand over the mark and shot a venomous look toward the backyard.

"Nikki again, huh?" he asked without missing a beat, used to our cheerleading injuries. "When's Carey due back?"

I blushed. "Next month," I said, at the same time Angel said, "Dad! We are NOT discussing boys with you. Out!"

She stood and pulled him to his feet, pushing him out of the room. He protested the entire way, but the huge grin on his face said he was messing with her. I hid a smile when Angel collapsed back beside me on the couch.

"Shut up, Q," she said, smacking my arm.

"What? I didn't say anything."

Angel scowled. "He's lonely. It's hard on him when Mom is gone this long."

I held out my palms. "I get it. You don't have to explain that to me. Besides, I love your dad. I want him to adopt me."

With a sigh, Angel pulled her legs up under her. "I'm not sure how you do it, Q. I can't imagine waiting around for some guy to come home. Wondering *if* he'll come home."

I shrugged. "Carey's not 'some guy.' That makes it easier. But yeah, I think it's going to be worse when he deploys. I know it will. Look at my mom."

Angel looked surprised. We didn't talk about my mom often. "You don't think you'd cheat like she did?"

"No! Geez, Ang!"

She didn't look sorry. "It happens. You know it happens."

Something about her seemed off. I couldn't put my finger on it. "Your dad didn't . . . ?"

Her eyes widened. "No! We both miss my mom a lot. I told you he's lonely." Then she added, "Besides, if he ever did, I'd never forgive him. I think cheating on someone who's risking their life for our country is pretty much the lowest of the low. I could never respect someone who did that."

Really, when I think about that night and what she said, I never should have expected her to stand by me when people thought I'd cheated on Carey.

Chapter Seventeen

Of all places to go, the laundry room seems the most ironic. For a girl who can't get clean, the garbage room would seem to be more fitting, but that would take feeling sorry for myself to a new low.

I'm not sure how I'll show my face upstairs in my hotel room. Or in public for the next few days.

Sitting on the floor of the guest Laundromat three floors below the one I'm assigned to, I bump my head against a washer and breathe air that smells like mildew and fabric softener. I hate that Jamie got to me with that crap about my mother. I didn't cheat on Carey, but . . . I used Blake, didn't I? What did that make me? Not innocent. Not guilty, exactly. Caught in a gray area, maybe.

The one thing I do know is that I can't give myself away again like that. I can't betray who was in the picture with me because Jamie's barb hit a little close to home.

Eventually, when I grow sick of my thoughts, I drag myself up and into the elevator. When the doors open on my floor, I'm surprised to find Angel hanging around in the hall, leaning against the fancy burgundy wallpapered wall.

She sees me and rushes forward. "There you are! Where have you been?"

I don't realize I'm angry at her until she reaches out to touch me.

"Hiding," I say. "Licking my wounds."

There's an edge to my voice that makes her pull back a little. She tucks a strand of blond hair behind her ear. "You sound mad at me."

I laugh without humor. "You think?"

She grabs my arm when I brush past her. "Wait a second! I didn't do anything. Jamie—"

I swing around on her. "No, you're right. You didn't do anything. You never do anything."

"What the hell is that supposed to mean?"

"I thought we were friends, Ang. Did I imagine that? How could you let her do that to me?"

"No, you didn't imagine it," she says quietly. "But what do you expect me to do?"

"I expect you to be better."

Her lips tighten. "Than who? Jamie? Or you? I didn't do this to you, Q. I'm not the one who cheated on Carey."

Neither did I. My mouth opens. Closes. Opens. I stare at the

EXIT sign above her head so she can't see the truth in my eyes.

"What?" she shouts. "What are you not saying?"

I can't say what I'm thinking, so I tell her what I'm feeling. "I never would have let somebody treat you like that. No matter what. Your friendship meant too much to me."

"I could say the same."

She sounds so pissed at me, and I don't get it. "What did I do to you, Ang?"

"You didn't talk to me! If you were thinking of cheating, why didn't you talk to me first? You knew how I felt about this. I told you how I felt. Maybe if we had talked, I could've helped you. Maybe . . ."

She blasts me until she runs out of breath. Pacing back and forth on that ugly forest green carpet, she goes on and on about how I let her down. How I lied to her. How I threw our friendship away. She sets me in my place. Part of me aches because some of it is true—I haven't told her anything, and maybe that was a betrayal of our friendship. Part of me is pissed, though, because I wish she'd stood by me anyway.

"I'm sorry," I say finally. "You don't know how sorry."

I scrape my hands through my hair, pulling it forward to hide that I want to cry. I'm surprised by how beaten down I sound. Even Angel hears it.

"Quinn . . ."

"I'm tired, Ang. And honestly, I don't think I can take much more today. Good night, okay?"

After a moment, she nods and walks away. I wonder if maybe I've been hoping too hard that our friendship could be fixed. Because this feels too broken to be put back together again.

The next day Mr. Horowitz and Mrs. Daniels, our government/economics teacher, steer us off the bus when we arrive at the National Mall. We trail after a tour guide to the Lincoln Memorial where a huge Lincoln stares off, permanently majestic and resolute. The tour moves us from monument to monument like herded cattle. The guide remains cheery, but our group grows more solemn with each war memorial we pass.

Some of us have lost family members. Some of us have family fighting now. None of us have been untouched.

At the Korean War Memorial, one wall reads *Freedom Is Not Free*. The cost in that war: 54,246 dead US soldiers. 103,284 wounded. 8,177 missing.

Stainless-steel soldiers march through the garden in full combat gear, their faces molded with weary determination. *Don*, I think, trailing my fingers down one massive soldier's cold cheek. Scared but dutiful; this is how I imagine Don looked with the picture of that dead soldier tucked in his pocket to remind him what was at stake.

We move on to the simple World War I Memorial followed by the more grandiose World War II Memorial. The first is a smaller, round structure with twelve pillars, and the second is constructed of fifty-six pillars in a huge plaza. The difference in size is striking. One war already fading in our memories, and the other still fresh. The World War II Memorial features a wall with 4,048 gold stars. Each star, our tour guide tells us, represents one hundred dead Americans. An inscription near the wall reads: *Here we mark the price of freedom.*

Amazing how the cost is always life. 404,800 dead. That's an entire city wiped off the face of the map.

We move on.

The last stop is the Vietnam War Memorial.

Two long black granite walls meet at a ninety-degree angle. Seventy panels listing 58,267 names. Columns of names. Rows and rows of names. Every single one a soldier who died or is MIA. No ranks are listed, and I guess this is because all men are equal in death. Equally dead.

Wandering away from the group, I use the directory to locate one name in particular. Charlie Deacon. George's friend who died when his helicopter got shot down over Laos. Before I left, he'd asked me for a favor—to find Charlie's name on the wall and take a picture of it. It seems like such a small thing to ask after everything he's given me.

49E, the directory says. The forty-ninth panel on the eastern wall. I find that panel and read down the list until I find Charlie close to the bottom.

I snap off a few shots and kneel down to touch the diamond engraved after his name, wondering what it means. I slide a pencil over Charlie's name, rubbing it into a piece of tracing paper

I brought with me. Something to bring back to George. Then I notice the engraving after Charlie's. Alex Petrov. Alex is a stranger, but he has a cross symbol instead of a diamond.

"It means he's MIA," a voice says from behind me.

I twist about, my finger still on the cross. Blake stands a couple of feet away with his hands in his pockets and his black hair tucked under a baseball cap. I raise a brow, and he tilts his head toward the wall.

"A diamond if the soldier's confirmed dead," he explains. "A cross if he's missing in action."

"Oh," I say, tracing the cross with my finger again. Alex Petrov has been missing for decades. His family never knew what happened to him. Maybe they still hope he will be found.

I touch Carey's class ring that hangs around my neck. He has to come home. I limp through each day knowing I'm in limbo—a limbo that ends when he tells the truth. Someday, none of this will matter. Not Jamie or Ang or my father. Some-day, when Carey returns, these days will be a shitty reminder of a time when we weren't the best versions of ourselves.

But "what if" won't go away. What if this is it—the best things will be? What if Carey is dead? What if we never know what happened to him? What if I can never tell Blake the truth about what I feel for him? Do you have to keep promises to dead people?

I hate myself for even wondering.

Blake's hand covers mine on the wall.

We are both thinking Carey's name. It hangs in the silence that is always between us.

The touch is meant to comfort. I know that. Yet . . . His breath heats my neck, and his thigh brushes mine where he crouches beside me. The black granite wall reflects our bodies. His eyes trained on me, he waits. If I turn my head, my lips will be near his.

I can't believe I'm thinking about kissing Blake again. Not here. Not now.

I tug until I free my hand. He lets me go, but when I try to run away, he blocks my path. Others begin to notice us together. The gossip about our dance at the Spring Fling died down when we ignored each other at school as usual. But this will make it start all over again. Yesterday's conflict at the elevator is too fresh.

"Blake," I say. "What part of 'stay away' didn't you understand?"

His shoulders square in determination. "We need to talk, Q. About Carey."

"No."

He puts his hands in his pockets and the muscles in his arms shift. Stupid guy wore a T-shirt and no coat, but he doesn't look cold.

"We talk later," he demands. "Or now, with everyone listening."

"Go to hell," I say. It worked before, but not this time.

His voice soft, he asks, "Aren't we already there, Q?"

He's pleading with me, but I don't owe him anything. Whatever damage I did by sleeping with him, I've made up for it a hundred times by keeping my mouth shut about the photo. I can't meet his gaze, so intense and full of things I only let myself think about when I'm alone. Those eyes steal the anger I should feel. That I do feel.

Over Blake's shoulder, I see Jamie watching us. I flip her off, tired of feeling bashed, then wish I hadn't given her the satisfaction of a response as she smiles like a cat. A big, predatory jungle cat hunting some poor, unsuspecting animal.

Blake turns and sighs when he sees her. "Why do you antagonize her? It only encourages her."

"You're kidding me, right?" I ask, crossing my arms. "She doesn't need encouragement. She hates me."

"You go out of your way to mess with her. You always have." He sounds like the old Blake, not giving me any slack, but it pisses me off because I'm not the old Q and he's not the old Blake. We're two used-to-be-friends who betrayed each other and made a huge mistake one night.

"Because she was always trying to steal my boyfriend!" He doesn't look happy that I've brought up Carey in that context, and I'm glad. I glare at him. "Why do you do this?"

"What?" he asks, confused.

"This," I say, gesturing between us. "Antagonize *me*."

I walk away, but he clasps my arm with just enough pressure to stop me. Finally, he's angry too.

"What are you talking about?"

"Hey, you two. Everything okay here, Quinn?" Mr. Horowitz approaches, a belated champion. He glances at me with concern. I can feel everyone pressing in closer to eavesdrop, and it's like yesterday with the room keys all over again.

"Sure," I say. Blake drops his hand and I add, "Just a friendly disagreement over Blake's hat." He's wearing an Atlanta Falcons cap that's offensive to any die-hard Carolina Panther fan. But he's one of the few guys at our school who could get away with wearing it.

Horowitz latches on to my explanation after I give a nod of reassurance. Enough of Sweethaven's population are rabid sports fans to make what I said plausible if not believable. My classmates—denied good gossip—react with disappointed sighs when he begins shepherding us all back to the bus.

Before I slip among them, Blake's fingers brush mine and he whispers to me, "I need to know what happened with Carey that night you came to my house. Please, Q."

Chapter Eighteen

Jamie gets her revenge that night, and I hate that Blake was right about antagonizing her.

After volunteering to get ice (anything to escape Night #2 in a fifteen-foot by fifteen-foot box shared with three other girls doing their best to ignore me), I'm locked out of our hotel room. I know it's not an accident. I figure it out after my fifth knock elicits a spurt of laughter from the room, and one of the mocking voices belongs to Jamie.

I seriously loathe high school and wannabe mean girls and idiotic field trips.

A quick walk down the hall to Mrs. Peringue's room and my roomies will be in a load of trouble. Then I could look forward to sleeping with my eyes open while Janet, Amery, and Danielle plot to do me in after a little prodding from Jamie. The others are not as malicious as she is, but Jamie has a way of looking like a leader to the clueless, and they're happy to follow. What's the point?

I sigh. Nothing to do but wait them out and hope they eventually let me in. No sense in desperately hanging out in the hall, though. Barefoot, I turn on my heel, taking the ice bucket with me. I hope they really wanted that ice and die of thirst.

A bellman eyes me when I step off the elevator, and I hold up the ice bucket and shrug as if to say, *My parents sent me to get ice. What're you going to do?* There's a sign for an indoor pool, so I head down the hallway. I test the door to the pool, thinking it will be locked, requiring a room key which I obviously don't have, but it opens under my touch.

The shrieks of two kids echo in the long, well-lit windowed room as they play Marco Polo in the shallow end of the pool. Their parents watch from a nearby table, but the room is otherwise empty. This seems as good a place as any to hang out for a while.

I pad to the edge of the deep end, set my ice bucket down, roll up my jeans, and plunk both legs into the heated water. Leaning back on my forearms, I stare out the wall of windows where my reflection is superimposed on the night skyline.

I'll give the girls an hour to get over their prank, and then I'll sick Mrs. Peringue on them. And then they'd better hope they don't fall asleep, because I have a camera and plenty of batteries. If I'm lucky, I'll catch them drooling. Hello, Yearbook. We'll see how they like having their pictures posted for the world to see.

"Hey. Mind if I join you?"

Blake stands over me in olive green board shorts and a T-shirt that says IF LIFE GIVES YOU MELONS, YOU MAY BE DYSLEXIC. I'm not even surprised to see him. It's that kind of night, that kind of week, that kind of life. I shrug, too tired to fight the overwhelming tide, and he sits, sinking his legs into the water too.

He nods at the ice bucket at my side. "What's up with that?"

"Fool's errand," I mutter. He looks confused. "Jamie. She and the others locked me out of our room."

He winces, but at least he doesn't say "I told you so." "Sorry."

"You should be," I say. My nasty tone startles him, but he relaxes when I add, "Now you're subjected to my ugly feet." I wave them, swirling the water. "My shoes are in the room, probably filled with lotion or toothpaste."

Straight-faced, he shakes his head in pity at my submerged legs, but his eyes smile. "You do have the ugliest feet I've ever seen. Your right pinkie toe creeps me out the way it looks like it'll swallow the others."

He's said this to me before, making Carey and me laugh while we lazed about his house watching TV. That day, he'd wiggled the toe in question and I'd fought back a shiver, pretending his touch had no effect on me. Now I shove him with one foot, splashing him a little.

"Shut up, jerk."

His laugh sands the rough edge inside me, and I smile.

He stills, staring at me in that intense way he does. "I missed that," he says finally, lifting his eyes from my mouth.

"What?"

"Your smile. You never smile anymore."

And just like that, reality dismisses my smile. "Yeah, well, I don't have a lot to smile about."

We're both silent then, watching the mother call her kids out of the pool. The family gathers their things, the youngest whining the whole way to the door about life not being fair. I swish one leg in a circle and then the other, watching the water ripple toward Blake in chaotic rings. How wrong is it that I missed the way he stares at me?

"I got a letter from Carey," I say without thinking.

He sucks in a breath, the only sign he's heard me, until I turn to look at him. He's choked up and way too happy about a simple letter. It hits me what he may be thinking—that Carey was found. I grab his hand.

"No! He sent it before he went missing."

In less than thirty seconds, I've managed to take him from joy to grief. He loves Carey like a brother and looks after Carey's parents as if he is their son. He turns his head to get himself under control and clenches his jaw so tight I can see the bones working.

"I'm sorry," I say when he swipes a hand across his face. "I didn't think about how that would sound."

He nods and squeezes my fingers. "No, I should've known better. I just . . . you know."

Wished for it so hard, you thought it might be true.

"Yeah, I know." I let him go.

"What'd he say?" he asks, changing the subject.

"That he missed us."

"That's it?" He bumps me with his shoulder and gives me a doubtful look. Carey tends to be long-winded in his letters.

"No. There was other stuff. Personal stuff."

Blake seems to guess I'm leaving the important things out. He searches my face for an explanation, but luckily he's not Carey who can read my thoughts.

"Before . . . when Jamie was giving you a hard time . . . you said he knew about the picture. He saw it, then? He knows it was me."

It's not a question, but I nod.

"The tattoo," I say slowly.

A longer answer isn't really necessary. The three of us got tattoos together before Carey left for basic, sneaking to Blake's tattoo-artist brother since my father would never have agreed to me getting one. Only three people in the world could recognize the ink on Blake's back. His brother, Carey, and me. His mom hated tattoos, so he'd purposely placed it low enough on his back that his clothes had to be coming off to see it. Say, like in a picture, with a half-naked girl all over him. I still don't know what the bird means to him. We'd all agreed that the tattoos had to mean something we could live with for a lifetime, but he wouldn't tell us about his.

"But . . ." He sounds puzzled, and I glance up to find him staring into space. "I talked to him, Q. We talked after the picture came out. He didn't say anything. Why?"

I shrug. "You'd have to ask him."

"What's going on? He acted like everything was fine with you."

Two guys and I love them both. Loyalty divides and subtracts me from both of them.

"We were friends before all this," he whispers. "That has to count for something."

Carey comes first. Right now, he has to come first. But there has to be a middle ground. What can I say without breaking my promise? I weigh my words.

"He doesn't have the right to be upset." *He's gay.* "I told you we broke up that night." That much is true.

For six months I've let Blake think that I lied to him the night we slept together. When I agreed to pretend to still be Carey's girlfriend, it seemed easier to let Blake think of me as selfish: a manipulative bitch who'd used him in some kind of game with Carey. Easier to let him hate me for using me, as if my heart hadn't been involved at all, than to admit I had to give him up for Carey. And how Blake hated me!

The kiss in that picture Jamie posted . . . it began so differently. It happened out of anger and frustration and Blake's need to prove that I cared about him. I'd shown up at the summer scrimmage as Carey's date, before he deployed, and Blake had pulled me under the bleachers. An argument about our night together turned into the kiss that was our last. If Blake had wanted to punish me for using him, it didn't work. The kiss became more than we expected. Something far more real.

I can't think about that, can't remember how much more I wanted. For months, I've shoved my feelings for Blake aside. It's hard to do that now, when he looks like I've punched him in the gut. The taut way he holds himself. Mouth turned down and drawn tight.

"You really broke up?" He leans forward in desperation when I won't respond.

This matters more to him than it should. Knowing I didn't lie that night doesn't change the fact that—in the world's eyes—I went back to Carey the next day. It's obvious that it does matter, though. All I can say is "Things aren't always what they seem."

His eyes pinch. I've hurt him. A lot.

This might be my breaking point. If anyone but Carey had asked me to keep this secret, I would tell. Right now. Because I want Blake like I've never wanted anything. But there's more at stake than my feelings.

An image of Carey's battered body floats in my memory. When he came to me asking for help and asking me to keep his secret, it wasn't words alone that swayed me. Nor did I make my promise lightly.

As for Blake, as far as he's concerned, I toyed with him. I slept with him and rejected him. Keeping my promise hasn't made me a saint. No, I'm fucked up and wishing I could have Blake, the one person I've hurt the worst.

Still, he lets me shoulder the blame alone.

"Why haven't you come forward?" I ask bitterly. "Confessed it was you in the picture?"

"You destroyed me, Q." Hurt rubs under the anger in his rough voice. "You knew I cared about you."

I'd guessed. The way he'd watched me had hinted at what he felt. Why else would I have driven to his house? I had something to prove to myself, and I knew he wouldn't refuse.

"You wanted me. Not him. *Me*." He's daring me to deny it, and I can't. "But the next morning, you ran away while I was sleeping and then you showed up at that damned game with him. Like we never happened." He drops his hand. "How could you fucking do that to me, Q?"

Shame swallows me, and I wish I could disappear into its belly. I did use him. At first.

"I'm sorry," I whisper, and the words aren't enough to make up for what I've done.

He turns away, and I can see his Adam's apple slide when he swallows. "Yeah . . . so am I. When Jamie posted that picture, I thought, 'Good. Let Q see what it feels like to be stabbed in the back.'"

Ouch.

He adds, "But then I saw how they were treating you . . . I meant to confess a long time ago. I really did."

"So what happened?"

"The Breens happened." He kicks a leg out, making a small splash. "They're not doing great. They fight all the time. Mrs. Breen kind of fell apart after Carey deployed. I'm doing everything I can to help them keep it together. Working at the shop extra hours, so Mr. Breen can spend more time at home. Taking care of things around their house, things Carey would do if he were here on weekends."

I imagine Carey's mother as I've seen her these last months. It's hard to picture her clearly when I've hardly been able to look her in the eye. Part of me hates that she hasn't guessed that I didn't cheat on Carey—she should know I'd never betray her son. The problem with looking down to avoid obstacles, though, is missing what's up ahead. I didn't see what Blake obviously has.

He continues. "When Mrs. Breen found out about the picture, she lost it. Carey refused to speak to any of them about you. He said they didn't know what they were talking about. She thought for sure he'd go off and get himself killed because he was upset about you. I couldn't tell her I'd betrayed him too. I couldn't do that to her. And now that he's missing . . . I promised him I'd take care of them if anything happened to him."

I wrap my arms around my waist, feeling sick. How frustratingly ironic.

I sacrificed Blake for Carey. Blake sacrificed me for Carey's parents. The whole thing is so screwed up. I don't know how to even begin to unravel the mess we've made.

"Why didn't you tell anyone it was me?" Blake asks. He gives me the same look he used to give me when I'd done something he thought was illogical. Like when Carey and I started dating years ago.

"Why, Q? If he knows, and you were broken up, why not tell everyone?"

His eyes are bleak and shadowed. We've really done a number on him, Carey and me. Blake isn't perfect—far from it—but he loves us. And I brought him into this mess, even if I didn't mean to.

"I made a promise to Carey, too." He opens his mouth, but I cut him off. "I can't tell you. Please don't ask. The thing is . . . if I say more, I'll be breaking that promise to him."

He thinks about that, and then Blake laughs. The raw, tired anger threading through it echoes in the room. "Damn, Carey."

I know what he means. Carey's at the heart of everything that's happened between us. Almost everything.

"I've got to go," I say. I pull my legs from the water and rise. Standing over him, I study the top of his head and wish things could be different.

He must be thinking the same thing because he looks up and says, "I'm sorry. If I could figure out a way to confess and keep my promise to Carey, I would. Tell me you know that."

"I do." On impulse, I lean over and touch his face, running my fingers over his shadowed jaw just to feel the scratch of his sandpaper whiskers. "You were wrong, you know."

"About what?" he asks, confused.

"I could never pretend that night never happened." I surprise him by bending over and kissing him. It's dangerous because I want more, but my loyalty is still with Carey. I let my lips tug on his for *one-two-three* seconds before I reel myself back in. "It meant too much."

Then I leave, taking my ice bucket with me, while he reaches for the place where I used to be.

Chapter Nineteen

George looks frail today. More so than usual.

Today's lesson—how to shoot a textured photo in dim light—creates deep valleys of frown lines on his forehead and neck. His room sits in shadows with the blinds cracked on one window so we can control the sunlight dancing on his food tray. He shifts from his wheelchair to the hard-backed chair at the table. I have to force myself not to help him when he groans in pain. My hands want to ready themselves to support him. My body tenses to catch him if he falls. The fact that he gets there on his own doesn't make it any less painful to watch.

George settles himself.

"You can relax now," he says with sarcasm. "I'm not going to keel over on you."

I load my sigh with drama and roll my eyes. "Don't give me a hard time, old man. I'm younger and meaner than you are."

I give up pretending not to care and grab a blanket off his bed. Crouching on my heels so I'm not standing over him, I toss the throw over his leg and glare up at him, daring him to say something.

So, of course, because he's George, he says something. "Your mama."

It takes a second to process. I pause, smoothing the blanket over his foot. Then I start laughing, really more of a snicker that turns into a chuckle, when he glowers at me from under furry eyebrows. I laugh harder, clutching my stomach, and he gives me a light shove that lands me on my backside on the tiled floor.

"Did you just bust out with 'Your mama' to insult me?" I mimic the proper way he said it, and he throws a napkin from his food tray at me. He tries to hide his smirk, and I squeeze his foot, giving him a pleading look. "Please, George. Please promise me you won't ever say that again. You're just not cool enough to carry it off."

My book bag sits on the floor nearby, and I remember the surprise I brought with me. "I have something for you."

"If it's a cheeseburger, medium-rare with grilled onions, I'll love you forever."

I shake my head. "You're not tricking me again. Nurse Espinoza yelled at me the last time."

He grins shamelessly. "Yeah, that was the best part."

I stick my tongue out at him and give him the package. George loves presents, no matter how small or lame they are.

I could bring him a bottle cap and he'd love it. He's like an overgrown kid ripping the small box open with more enthusiasm than care. He pulls the tissue paper aside and pauses, his hand hovering over the gift. It only measures about seven inches by two inches. The frame is a silly one I made from heavy cardboard I'd found at the craft store and painted with red, white, and blue stripes. An old cut-up army-green canvas bag of my dad's serves as the matte for the rubbing I did of Charlie Deacon's name.

I thought George would smile and chuck me under the chin with thanks, but he doesn't. Instead, he traces the diamond after Charlie's name. He knows what that symbol means. His entire body wilts with an old, remembered sadness. Then tears begin a silent slide down his cheeks.

I've never seen George cry.

George camouflages his vulnerability in irritability. If I try to help him too much, he snarls at me. Leave him alone, and I'll feel like a crappy friend for deserting him. What to do? Stay or go? I think about the times I've cried, and the way he'd awkwardly patted my hand.

I pull a chair beside him and wait.

He studies the rubbing for a long time.

"Charlie," he says finally, his voice ragged. "Man, I hated Charlie Deacon."

He sees how shocked I am and laughs. "You should've seen this guy. Six-foot-four, red-headed, and the biggest redneck I've ever met. He picked fights with the wind if it turned the wrong direction."

George sinks back against his chair to gaze at the ceiling's acoustic tiles.

When George doesn't continue, I say, "I thought he was your friend."

He's quick to answer. "Hell no. I hated that big bastard. His temper got me and the guys into more brawls . . . One time," he says, his tone a weird cross between anger and amusement, "one time he bet this jarhead he could stitch up a knife wound faster than a medic. Damned if he didn't slice his own leg open and sew it closed without anesthesia to win that bet."

George snorts and adds, "I thought I'd be lucky to make it out of 'Nam alive with Charlie at my back." He absently rubs his leg.

A crash cart rolls by, and we watch in silence as a white coat rushes behind it. Urgent voices blaze down the hall. Funny enough, I don't know many of the patients on George's floor. We spend most of our time outside or in common areas. I think George considers the floor a cancer, an outgrowth of the one inside him. He hates to be reminded of death.

"So what happened?" I ask.

He sets the gift box on the table. "Well, now, we were stationed at this airfield at Cu Chi. Not bad as far as base camps go. But this one night, the enemy sneaks on base. Before we can even think about getting to our weapons, they're firing RPGs and bullets are spitting at everything that moves. One guy's on his way to take a shower when he's killed."

George continues, "Me and Charlie, we huddled down behind sandbags in front of our hootch with our forty-fives. Later on we found out they were out to destroy our Chinooks—helicopters—and they got nine of them. Along with fourteen men."

I've heard others at the VA talk about their war experiences, but George hasn't said much. He mostly listens and asks questions. Sometimes he offers comfort. I try to picture him as a young man, scared of dying. He couldn't have been much older than Carey when he fought.

"Anyway," he says. "I get this bright idea to run toward the helos, thinking maybe I can take a couple of these guys out. I was such a dumb-ass wanting to be a hero, and I knew some of my buddies were out there. Damned if I didn't run into a sapper the first corner I rounded. He had me dead to rights, and I thought, 'This is it. I can kiss my ass good-bye.' The gun went off, and guess who showed up in the nick of time?"

He gestures toward the frame. "Charlie Deacon took a round to the head saving my life."

What makes one person do that for another? How do you decide to sacrifice your life for someone who doesn't even like you? It makes no sense.

"Maybe he thought you were a friend," I suggest.

"Hell no," George says with another laugh. "Charlie hated me as much as I hated him."

He stares, the unseeing kind of stare that looks inward.

"Why would he do that?"

A half-smile forms on his face and he shrugs. "That's war, kid. You can hate the guy next to you, but he's always got your back."

The look on George's face is too intense, too private, and I look away. Charlie, a red-headed redneck, died a hero. The reason? Soldiers die for their brothers. Carey would do the same for the men in his battalion. I know he would. The boy who let a drunk pound him into a diner's floor to save a girl grew into a man who would risk everything to help others.

But where do I rate? Somewhere between Carey's brothers and the gum stuck to the bottom of his shoe. Isn't he letting me take the bullet for him? How could he sacrifice me like that? I'm not sure why I'm surprised. I know better. My own father chose country and brotherhood over our family.

"What's on your mind?" George says.

Anger overrides my instinct to keep my mouth shut. "Can I ask you something?"

"Shoot."

"What the hell is with this brotherhood bullshit? You and Charlie hated each other, but he died protecting you. And Carey . . ." I stop. I swallow my words before I say too much.

"What did Carey do to you?"

It's the first time he's asked me what happened, point-blank. It's the first time someone suspects Carey is behind what's wrong with me. I keep quiet, though it kills me.

"So stubborn, Sophie. You keep holding all that anger in and it'll eat you up." He sighs. "Help me up, would you? My hip hurts sitting in this damn chair."

We work together to maneuver him from the chair to the bed. I help him settle in, tucking the blanket around him and fixing his pillows. For once, he doesn't give me a hard time for helping him. We watch TV, neither of us laughing at the funny parts of the *Family Guy* rerun.

A commercial comes on and I say, "What if you'd been gay?" I study the advertisement for a dishwashing soap like my life depends on it, feeling George's gaze as a physical weight. "Do you think Charlie would've taken that bullet for you then?"

The silence goes on for so long I don't think he's going to answer. Finally he says, "I honestly don't know. Charlie hated anyone who was different. Not a lot of folks let on back then. I do know this: Some guys would've taken me out to the paddies and beat me until I wished I was dead rather than sleep two feet from me."

George never bullshits me. He doesn't give me the answer I want—that Charlie would have taken that bullet come hell or high water. He doesn't lie, either. Times haven't changed all that much. Proof of that was all over Carey's battered body the night he convinced me to lie for him.

George confirms what I'm thinking. "You know, even today I'd think twice before coming out. Aside from the honorable discharge, all you'd get for your honesty is some homophobic macho asshole wiping the latrine with you."

The show comes back on, and we watch Stewie and Brian argue.

When you think about it, the military isn't so different from screwed-up families everywhere. Sacrifice everything, including your life, and it still isn't enough. At the end of the day, you have to lie about who you are if you want to survive. *Be all you can be. Aim high. The few, the proud. Don't ask, don't tell.* What crap.

"Some brotherhood," I say.

The bed squeaks, and I hear George sigh. "Nobody's perfect," he says, his voice weighted with sadness. "We're all just doing the best we can."

I know that. I do. But lately, it doesn't seem like it's enough.

Chapter Twenty

Blake and I don't suddenly become friends again. Whatever happened between us at the pool, we leave it behind in DC. I can't tell the truth and he has his own promise to keep. The day after we get home I pass Carey's mother in the hall, and I can't even blame Blake for choosing her over me. She's hollow, her stare blank, as if her insides have been scraped out, leaving only seeds of sorrow and dread behind. The longer Carey's MIA, the less likely it is that he will return. Mrs. Breen breathes this reality every single minute, and it looks like it's killing her.

On the brighter side, when I turn in the senior trip photos, Mr. Horowitz beams and announces to the Yearbook staff, "People, Quinn has saved us! Finally, some photos we can use!"

Jamie's face turns a shade of soured milk, and I want to pump my fist in victory. Not my finest moment, but she did humiliate me with that key thing and get me locked out of my hotel room. She's lucky I didn't turn in a shot of her with her lipstick smeared from kissing Jimmy Manning in the back of the bus. If I hadn't decided to use my power of photography for good, blackmail would be on the table. The last bell rings and I barely restrain myself from smirking as I walk past her to head home.

My father's standing on the porch when I pull into the driveway. He's leaning against the railing with his arms crossed over his chest as he glares at his barren garden. Guilt makes my cheeks hot, and I take my time gathering my book bag so I can steady my nerves before I reach him. I should tell the truth about what I did, switching his weed killer and plant food. I won't, though. Since that nightmare I had about Carey, he doesn't seem to hate me like before. I'm not willing to give that up. His garden can take the blow; I can't.

Tossing my bag over my shoulder, I take the steps to the porch. "Hey, Dad."

"Quinn."

He sounds distracted, and I continue past him to the door. I'm reaching for the doorknob when he stops me. "What do you think about going out to dinner tonight? I thought we could grab a bite at the diner."

I hesitate. We haven't been out to dinner since the picture came out, like he's been ashamed to be seen with me in public.

"Are you sick?" It's the only explanation I can think of.

He frowns. "Of course not. I just thought it would be nice not to cook. How about it?"

"Sounds good." I feel like a shaken soda can. We're turning a corner, and it's anyone's guess what's waiting around the bend. Based on past experience, it'll be a brick wall. I leave him to ponder the mystery of his dead garden.

Later, we climb into my father's truck and spend an awkward ten minutes driving to the diner. We've forgotten how to speak to each other. He knows next to nothing about me—at least none of the important stuff. I don't want to talk about his job or the military or Carey.

We settle on the weather. I'm not sure who brings it up first, but we both latch on to it.

"I think we're going to get some rain this weekend."

"It's pretty cold out."

"Summer's probably coming late."

"I'll be glad when it warms up."

Brilliant.

Inside Sweethaven Café, the scent of thirty years of burnt coffee, bacon grease, and cigarette smoke greet us. Michelle Lovell hasn't allowed smoking in the café in years, but the stench lingers though people no longer tap their ashes into ashtrays. If it wasn't our only option for a night out in town, I'm not sure anyone would come here.

Veronica Lovell greets us at the hostess station, her nutmeg hair twisted back with a clip, a once-white apron tied around her waist. She graduated last year. We'd been friends, but I haven't seen much of her since she left for college in August. She'd managed a hefty scholarship with her grades, as her mom, Michelle, had proudly told everyone who walked into the café last year. Last I heard, she was living in Boston.

She surprises me with a smile and a hug when she sees me. "Hey, Q."

I hug her back a little tighter than I should. She's genuinely happy to see me, and I wonder if the gossip has somehow bypassed her. "Hey, Ronnie. What're you doing back here?"

Her nose wrinkles, folding her freckles together, and she leads us to a booth. "I'm taking a semester off. Dad broke his leg, and he and Mom needed me home to help out."

Her father is cook, while her mom runs the front. Without help, her parents could easily lose the café.

I touch her elbow. "I'm so sorry. I didn't know."

She shrugs and brushes away her brown bangs with her forearm. "What're you gonna do?"

My father and I slide into opposite sides of the booth, and Ronnie hands us menus. Before she leaves, she says, "Not a lot of vegetarian options on the menu, Q, but I'll see if my mom can throw together some veggies and pasta for you."

"That'd be great. Thanks, Ronnie."

The diner is busy tonight, and I open the menu to escape the eyes I feel eating us up.

"What was that about?" my father asks. He nods toward Ronnie and adds, "The vegetarian thing."

Uncomfortable, I shift in my seat, tucking a leg underneath me. "I don't eat meat."

My father sits on his side of the booth, and nothing about him looks relaxed. Perfect posture, perfect regulation hair, perfect record, imperfect daughter. I'm the weight throwing his life out of balance.

For so long, he avoided looking at me. Now, he stares like I'm an alien being. Someone replaced his perfect daughter with this thing I've become, and he doesn't know how it happened or what to do with me.

"Since when?" Skepticism rounds out the question.

Squaring my shoulders, I say, "Since we took a field trip to that farm."

I'm not sure who's bright idea that trip had been, but one look at the chicken slaughterhouse had pretty much decided it for me. Carey had teased me for weeks.

Ronnie drops a basket of bread on the table and walks away in a hurry when my father frowns at her.

"That was more than a year ago," he says.

"Yes, sir."

"Why didn't you say anything?"

He sounds angry, and I toy with a breadstick from the basket. *Because I kept waiting for you to see me.* "How could you not notice?"

It's the closest I've come to disrespecting him. His wintergreen eyes narrow, and I can't tell what he's thinking. I am saved by Ronnie returning to take our order. A salad and the pasta for me, and a burger for him.

He crosses his arms over his chest. The way he's focused on me is disconcerting after having been ignored for so long. It's a struggle to keep myself from fidgeting. Finally he says, "I really don't know you anymore, do I?"

I can't be sure, but I think he sounds a little sad. "I didn't think you wanted to. Not after . . ."

I can't say Carey's name. His name has this power now to kill the joy in any room. What if saying it reminds my father to hate me?

He's silent, and I'm disappointed. At least he doesn't lie and deny the truth, though. Our food arrives and it could be any other night at our kitchen table. He asks me about my homework and school, and I give my usual answers of "Done" and "Fine." I peer at my plate to avoid the curious stares I imagine.

When my plate is clean, I wipe my mouth with a napkin and catch my father eyeing my empty plate. His lip curls in a small smile.

"That's the most I've seen you eat in months. I guess now I know why."

Humor laces his tone, and I can't hide my shock.

He props an arm over the back of the booth. "You could've told me, you know. I wouldn't have forced a steak into you."

I take a chance on his lighter mood. "But then Rueger wouldn't be so fat and happy."

His eyes widen as he makes the connection between the dog's round body and my half-eaten dinners. I wait for the anger to resurface, but he surprises me again by laughing.

"Carl's had him on a diet for weeks," he says. "He can't understand why Rueger's gaining weight."

He laughs again, and I join in. How long can this last, the two of us getting along? Especially once the blame starts flowing again. What if this cease-fire makes it more painful to withstand the next battle? I sober up. I'm not sure I can handle that.

My father reaches for my hand and I yank it back without thinking, closing ranks to protect myself. He looks sad, but not surprised, at my response.

"I'm trying, Quinn," he says, tossing some money on the table to cover the check.

Trying to make up for the way he's treated me? Trying to be nice for a change? I'm not sure what the answer is, and I've been trying to be indifferent after he cut me for too long to act otherwise.

On our way to the door, my father is stopped by one of his work buddies. Sergeant McIntosh and he start talking base politics and I lose interest in seconds. A table near the window catches my attention.

Blake and Angel sit across from each other. They've never really been friends, and seeing the two of them together hits me like an out-of-body experience. He leans toward her in an intimate way that makes me want to scream. Without meaning to, I walk toward them, and I'm right on top of their table before they notice me. Angel's quiet voice comes to a halt.

Blake pulls away from her suddenly, and if I wanted to, I could read it as guilt. Except that we aren't together. In fact, less than a week ago, he told me how much he'd hated my guts for what I did to him. And haven't I hated him, too, for letting me take the blame for an angry kiss he instigated?

"Hey," Angel says. "How's it going?"

Her voice has none of the anger it had that night in the hotel, and I don't know what to make of it.

"Good," I answer, not meaning it.

"You came here alone?" She sounds a little incredulous. Honestly, I would never think of coming here alone.

I gesture over my shoulder to where my father is shooting the breeze with his friend. "No. My father and I had dinner."

"Ah," she says. "That makes more sense."

Blake still hasn't said anything. I wonder if these two are dating now. He didn't mention it in DC, but then, why would he? It's not as if we owe each other anything. But Blake doesn't even say hi, and something in me won't let him ignore me.

"How's Mrs. Breen, Blake?"

"Okay, I guess. The same."

Not good, then. I already knew that, though, based on what I've seen of her. I can't think of anything else to say to Blake or Angel, and it's too late anyway. My father calls my name, and he's waiting by the front door.

"I've got to go. Later."

I turn, but Angel grabs my hand. "I saw the pictures you took of the senior trip. They're really good, Q."

It's not a lot, but it's something. I smile and squeeze her fingers. "Thanks, Ang. See you around."

She lets me go, and I force myself not to look at Blake.

Maybe, just maybe, it's time for me to stop looking backward.

Chapter Twenty-One

Escaping the past isn't as easy as I'd like it to be.

The next day at the hospital, I have a long visit with George in the atrium. There's a new tension to our time together now, since he told me about Charlie. I suspect he's waiting for me to confess the truth about Carey. I care about George, but he'll wait forever if he thinks I'll talk about the secret I'm keeping.

We are frustrated with each other. It shows in his impatience with me during our lesson and in my bad attitude when he tells me I'm framing a shot wrong. I want to tell him to back off, that our time together is my escape from all the other crap I have to put up with. He's my one person free from any connection to Carey. But I don't say anything. I don't want to hurt George's feelings by snapping at him when I know he just wants to help me.

After our lesson, I push his chair back to his room. He's giving me the silent treatment, and I'm tempted to ruffle his hair to mess with him. I give in to the urge, and he turns to scowl at me.

"Brat," he says.

I smirk. "Grouch."

He hits the brake on his chair. Walking full steam ahead, I can't stop in time and end up ramming into the back of the chair. Childish but effective. Score one for George.

We both snicker.

"Sophie?"

I look up guiltily, expecting one of George's nurses to reprimand us for goofing off.

My mother stands ten feet away. She clasps her hands to her mouth as if to hold in a sob. Her blue eyes water.

George has to wonder who she is, but I can't find the words to explain. I have no idea what to do, caught between fight or flight. A warm, calloused hand clasps mine and steadies me.

"Mom," I say, and it's amazing how frigid my voice sounds.

She wants to rush me. To hug me. I can see it in the tight way she carries herself, as if she's at the starting line of a race before the gun goes off. I'm glad she holds herself together because I don't know what I'd do if she tried to hug me.

"Sophie," she says again, and the tears hanging on her lashes fall.

"Stop crying," I demand. My words are harsher than I intended, but something about her tears pisses me off. What does she have to cry about? She got the life she wanted, didn't she?

"I'm George." He wheels toward her, holding out a hand for her to shake.

She reaches out her hand to shake his, but he clasps it instead. I know he's acting as peace keeper for me, but I hate that he's so gentle with her.

"Nice to meet you, George. I'm Sophie Quinn."

He grins at her in wonder. "Is that right? You and Sophie have the same name."

"Except for our middle names," I interject. "Mine's Topper, after my sainted uncle."

I want to add a lot more to that statement, but not in front of George. Lucky Mom. Little blisters of rage bubble up all over my body.

My mom gives me this uncertain look. "Yes, well . . . It's so good to see you, Sophie. I've missed you."

Right. Sure you have. I focus on a spot somewhere over her head.

She adds, "Can I speak with you? Alone?"

I'm about to refuse her when George steps in again. "Of course you can! I'll go ahead and get out of your way. Sophie here was just saying how much she wanted a cup of joe."

I ball my hands into fists. I hadn't said any such thing, and the interfering geezer knows it.

My mother takes a tentative step in the direction of the cafeteria. George rolls his chair close to me and gives me an encouraging smile, but his voice is iron rebar. "Go on, now. It's just coffee, kid."

He knows my mother walked out on us. I've told him that much. I can't believe how pushy he's being. "George—"

"You're in control here. Be nice."

It would be easy to pretend I don't know what he means. But George isn't the type to let me off the hook. I throw another glance at my mother. She's staring at us. It's painful to see her so vulnerable, filled with such open hope and wanting. I could walk away. I already did it once at the café. Again, George's presence stops me. He believes in me. Believes I'm better than everyone in town's made me out to be. Damn it.

"Fine," I bite off. I stalk past him and smack the elevator button. My mother follows me when the doors open. Before they close, George mouths *Be nice* and I almost flip him off.

"The canteen's on the first floor," I toss into the awkward silence.

"I know," she answers.

Thank God for elevator music. I'd have to slit my wrists if there wasn't something to study besides her. On the first floor, she trails after me, and it strikes me how different this is. When I was little, she charged everywhere, blazing a trail I couldn't keep up with.

We order our cappuccinos and I realize I left my purse in George's room. It kills me that she buys my $1.50 cup of crappy coffee. I don't want to owe her anything. I grab a table by the window, and she sits across from me. Outside, it's started to rain.

"Thanks for coming," she says.

"Thank George," I answer, and I can see the words cut her.

She gathers herself and tries to smile. It's a dismal failure. "Edward said you were angry."

I hate that she says his name. In my head, "Edward" stole her. But when she says his name, there is tenderness. It feels . . . apart from me and the life we had. Like there is more to her than I remembered or imagined.

"He mentioned you saw me before in the lobby. I wish you'd said something."

I sip my coffee and it scalds my tongue.

"Are you not going to talk to me?"

I sigh. "What do you want me to say? Do you want me to forgive you for walking away?"

Bingo. That's exactly what she wants. I can see it in her eyes.

"Fine. You're forgiven."

Abandoning my coffee, I rise to leave. She reaches for me and I flinch. She's left with her hand hanging in midair.

"Please, Sophie. Don't go."

I pause. I sink back into my seat, slouching with my hands in my sweatshirt pockets. I feel manipulated and pissed off and so freaking hurt I can't breathe. Against my will, I begin to cry. "You have no right to come here. I've done okay without you."

"I didn't," she says, her voice breaking. "I didn't do well at all."

"Didn't you?" I ask with venom. "You had no problem leaving me at Grandma's. You walked away like I was crap you couldn't get off your shoes fast enough."

"No! It wasn't like that at all."

"What was it like, then?" My raised voice draws eyes to our table, but for once, I don't care. Let them look.

My mother tucks her hair behind her ear in a gesture I don't remember. Her hair was too short to do that when I knew her. She must have a thousand habits I don't know about. Her choice, not mine.

"It's complicated," she says.

I laugh. "Seriously? That's what you're going with?" I strike a fist on the table and she jumps. "Thank goodness you explained yourself. I feel so much better now."

She folds her hands and stares at them.

"That's all you have to say?" I ask incredulously. "I'm not eleven anymore, in case you haven't noticed."

She takes a deep breath. "You're right, of course. I don't know where to start."

I plant both elbows on the table. "How about you begin with how you could leave me behind?"

I've thought about this for so long. Obsessed over it. Fantasized about reasons important enough to make her give me up. In my imaginings her reason always came down to life or death. If not for something so huge, she would never have considered leaving me. That's what I told myself anyway.

Perhaps some of my heartbreak seeps through the cracks in my voice because she reaches for me again. This time I let her hand rest on my arm.

"It wasn't about you, Sophie. I had to leave for myself. I was dying in that house, always waiting for your father to return. It was me or him, and I chose me."

She means it. The sincerity pours from her. She doesn't even realize how her explanation sounds to me. Mothers are supposed to put their children first: She chose herself. An ache starts deep in my chest, pressing on my lungs until I feel like I won't ever be able to breathe again.

"You have no idea what it was like after you left," I say quietly. "At first, I didn't realize you weren't coming back. When it finally hit me, I cried for days and days. Then the nightmares started."

"Soph—"

"Dad had no idea how to comfort me. He was so lost himself. It took months for us to figure out how to live without you. And another year after that for me to accept you had left for good."

She drops her hand, and I'm glad. Since that picture of Blake and me came out, people—my friends, my father, *me*—have compared me to her. Sophie Topper Quinn, an unfaithful slut like her mother. Sitting before her, I can see it's not true. I'm nothing like her.

I would never walk away from someone who needed me. I stay. Even when things get bad, I stay.

Maybe I am my father's daughter, after all.

"I think you should go," I tell her. *It's what you're good at.*

The finality in my tone sinks in. She abandons her coffee and stands. "I know you don't believe me, but I really did miss you."

"You're right," I say, staring up at her. "I don't believe you. You could've visited anytime. You didn't. Like you said, you chose you."

Her eyes widen, and pride straightens her back. "That's not fair. I tried to visit."

"Not hard enough," I say flatly.

"Your father said—" She stops, biting off whatever she intended to say.

"My father said what?" I had no idea they spoke after she left.

She tenses, her face twisted with frustration or anger. I can't tell which. When she does speak, she ignores my question. "I'm not going anywhere. Edward and I have moved back to North Carolina." She drops a piece of paper on the table. "That's my number. If you decide you want to see me."

I ignore her and she finally takes a hint. I sense her walk away, but I don't turn to watch her go.

Once was enough to last me a lifetime.

Chapter Twenty-Two

I've never felt so disgusted with myself as I did the morning I woke up in Blake's bed. I knew I'd made a mistake before I even opened my eyes. His body curved against my back, warming me where we touched. I lay there, confronting what I'd done and who I'd done it with. I'd used him.

Perhaps I should have been disoriented, wondering if it was Carey that I'd finally fallen into bed with. After all, I'd been dating him for two and a half years. But there was no mistaking the feel of that arm lying across my waist. Even in his sleep, Blake sent intense waves of emotion crashing through me. The night before, I'd welcomed all of it—the intensity and the heat. In the light of day, it overwhelmed me.

It took a full minute to slide out from under his arm, moving in millimeters to avoid waking him. I dragged my clothes and sorry self into the bathroom, relieved beyond belief when I didn't bump into Blake's brother on the way. Thank goodness his mother was out of town too.

Dressed in last night's tank top and jeans and disgusted with myself, I wondered what I would say to Blake. If there were magical words to make this all go away without ruining the friendship we had. Then a new, unwelcome thought popped in.

Did I really want to forget last night happened?

Did I want to pretend I hadn't seen a different side of Blake— a side of him that made me want to be the sort of girl that could inspire longing in his eyes? I could be that girl. Dangerous. Exciting. Something more than the goody-two-shoes, do-the-right-thing machine I'd become. Angel would never believe I'd gone to Blake after what happened with Carey last night. I almost couldn't believe it myself.

Yet, I considered going back into Blake's room and waking him to see if his kiss would feel the same in the morning light.

That's when my phone rang.

I snagged it out of my pocket, nearly dropping it in the sink in my hurry to silence the ringer.

"Hello," I whispered, expecting it to be my father checking up on me. Lucky for me, he would never know I'd stayed out all night since he's stayed overnight on base. I'm not sure I would have survived that icy blizzard.

"Quinn, don't hang up!"

Carey.

My gut twisted in a double knot. I had no idea what to say

to him. The night before, he'd shredded me with his confession. This morning, I'd woken up in his best friend's bed. Words failed me, so I said nothing and listened to him breathe on the other end of the line.

He took that as a good sign and continued. "I need to talk to you. Meet me?"

I didn't answer for the longest time. Anger should have been my strongest feeling, but the night before had confused me, sending my emotions winding through a blender.

Standing there in Blake's bathroom, staring at my disheveled reflection, I didn't know how I felt.

"Please, Quinn," he begged.

We couldn't leave things like we had last night. Not with him deploying in a few short days. *Better get this over with,* I thought. Rip off the Band-Aid.

"Where?"

Thirty minutes later, I parked my Jeep at the edge of Grave Woods. I felt like hell for sneaking out of Blake's house. I thought about leaving a note, but what could I say?

Hey, thanks! It was a blast. We should totally do it again. JK! I was just trying to feel better about myself and now I'm completely confused about my feelings.

Yeah, that would have gone over great. So I left Blake asleep in his bed and tiptoed out the front door.

I didn't feel any better when I neared the cemetery in Grave Woods and found Carey waiting with his back to me. He'd heard me coming. I could tell by the intent way he cocked his head. Basic had changed him. He had a new alertness about him. A readiness to launch into action, as if he could handle whatever came his way. He'd always been confident. Cocky, even, about his physical ability, especially on a football field. But this quiet confidence was the sort that came from knowing you could handle yourself in a knife fight. The Marines could transform a person in that way. I'd seen it time and again in our town.

Carey the boy had left for basic training; Carey the man had returned in his place.

I didn't know what to make of either of them.

"I went by your house again last night," he said, his arms hanging loosely at his sides.

He evaluated me, trying to figure out where he stood. I'd taken that look for granted for years. The way he always paid such close attention to my needs and wants. He had a way of reading me, and I wondered if he could tell how I'd changed since he'd made his confession on the porch the night before. Would he even care? Maybe I should have considered why he'd been so attentive and asked for nothing in return. Perhaps a guilty conscience for lying to me?

"Yeah?" I said with belligerence.

He didn't react to my snotty tone, but answered mildly, "I was worried. I upset you last night."

I didn't explain myself or tell him where I'd been. Maybe I'd made a mistake last night, but I no longer owed him anything. He'd betrayed me, not the other way around.

"Of course you upset me. Geez, Carey, you lied to me for ages."

He tilted his head in acknowledgment. "I know it doesn't make things any better, but I didn't mean to. That's the last thing I wanted to do."

I wanted to rage at him and make him feel as bad as I had. His apology and its obvious sincerity deflated my desire to shriek the forest down around him.

"You're right. It doesn't make things better." I sighed, sinking to sit on the ground.

I know Carey, and I could see he wasn't going to give me what I wanted—a screaming fight. He would let me yell at him, but he wasn't going to engage. He'd already taken the blame and would accept what I dished out. Damn it.

"I hate you," I said.

He gave me a half-smile, folding to sit near me, his back to Thomas's headstone. "No, you don't. You're mad at me and you're hurt, but you don't hate me."

He sounded so positive.

"What makes you so sure?"

"You're my best friend, Quinn," he answered with a shrug.

I slid forward onto my knees and slugged him as hard as I could in the shoulder. He let me do it. Didn't even try to stop me. Crying angry tears, I sat back again, shaking out my throbbing hand.

"You're such an asshole," I said, sniffing.

He nodded. "You're right. Hit me again if you want. I can take it."

Crying harder, I shook my head. "I don't know you. I thought I did, but it was all a lie, wasn't it?"

"Aw, Quinn . . ." He scooted closer to me. As if he knew the reception he'd get, he didn't try to touch me, but he dipped his head to look me in the eye. "I love you. I didn't lie about that. You and me, we're more than last night."

"You broke my heart," I whispered.

"Did I?" he asked. His dark gaze wouldn't let mine loose, as if he was daring me to tell the truth. Something we hadn't done a lot of in a while, I realized. "You knew something wasn't right with us."

"No!"

He gave me a disappointed look. "Who's lying now?"

"Shut up, Carey! You don't get to be the upset one here!"

"You're right," he conceded again.

"Stop saying I'm right!" I shouted.

Cracks began to show in his calm surface, and he exhaled a frustrated breath. "I'm doing the best I can here. What do you want me to say?"

"The truth!" I'd had enough lies.

"Ask me a question, then!" he said, anger thrumming in his words.

I stopped. My mouth opened and closed several times. I couldn't think of a single question that I wanted him to answer.

"You don't *want* to know the truth, Quinn! It's easier to just be pissed at me, isn't it?"

He stood and stalked away from me. If it had only been anger in his eyes, I could have dealt with that. Anger for anger. But pain blanched his face. That was harder to ignore.

"How long have you known?"

My quiet question sounded loud in the crisp morning air.

He didn't pretend to misunderstand. "A long time."

"Why me?" My voice broke on the question, and he struggled to meet my eyes. "Two years you led me on, letting me think we had a future. That's unforgivable, Carey."

"Don't you know how much I wanted that to be my future?" He spread his arms out wide. "Look at me! Do you think this is what I want? I'm in the military, for fuck's sake! 'Don't ask, don't tell.' What kind of life is that?"

"The one you've been living the past two years," I accused. "I didn't ask; you didn't tell."

My words hit him harder than my fist. I could see it in the way he flinched.

"You were wrong not to tell me."

His chin dropped to his chest, the picture of shame.

It wasn't enough. I wanted answers, not regret. "Why didn't you?"

"I was scared."

I rose and walked forward until I could feel his breath on my face. "Of what?"

He leaned toward me, resting his forehead against mine. "Losing you. We're the perfect couple, right? What would I do without you, Quinn? You hold me together."

I sighed. I knew what he meant. Once, during a football game, he'd taken a hard blow to the head from a huge linebacker. For a while, the doctors thought Carey might have some permanent vision damage. He'd been destroyed, thinking he wouldn't be able to enlist after graduation. I'd held his hand through that crisis and others. We'd always gotten each other in a way others didn't, even before we started dating. I couldn't imagine losing him.

"Idiot."

"I'll apologize until you forgive me. You'll see how I wear you down."

And he would, too. Like water against stone. My insides twisted in a kaleidoscope of disappointment, anger, and sadness. Each emotion crystalline in its intensity, but no one emotion stronger than the others. My own reaction confused me. One thing was clear: I felt stupid.

"You didn't answer my question. Do I have a target on my back? A sign that says 'This loser's gullible'?" I sounded pathetic. But how could I not have seen it?

Carey stroked my hair, tugging on a strand. "It wasn't like that, Quinn. It took me a long time to accept that this isn't something I can wish away or shut off. If I could choose anyone, it would be you."

"Except you're not attracted to me."

"That's not really a choice."

I stepped away from him, but he tugged on my hand and continued, "Besides, if you're honest, I think it goes both ways."

I was quiet for the longest time. Yesterday, I would have denied his words until I was blue in the face. Then last night happened. Blake happened. His arms and the spidery thrill that webbed through me when his fingers trailed over my skin.

I'd never felt that for Carey.

I looked at him. Really looked at him. At his dark hair and dark eyes. Handsome and confident. His sturdy strength appealed to me, but that wasn't the same as attraction. 'Security' wasn't a word that made my heart beat faster.

His brows raised as he read my face. "Wow. You *really* don't want me."

I considered telling him about Blake, but part of me rebelled. The memory of our night together belonged to me, and I wasn't willing to share it. But if I chose to tell anyone, it would have been Carey. When something happened to me, small or big, I told him. He was my person. Somehow, his revelation shifted everything except that. The knowledge came over me in a slow, painful crawl.

He'd hurt my pride and my feelings. I could punish him for hurting me. Or I could try to move past this.

Carey's fingers sweated in mine. My silence made him nervous. I could feel it. Stepping outside myself, I tried to understand him. How scared he'd been to tell me the truth. How scared he still was that I'd reject him, despite his best efforts.

How much was our friendship worth to me?

I finally answered his question. "Well, I've been meaning to tell you, you really are ugly as sin."

I'd surprised him into a laugh. "Shut up, Quinn."

"No, seriously," I protested. "Think Shrek. You're like a half-step removed from being his ogre twin."

My voice was muffled by his chest as he pulled me into a bear hug, resting his chin on the top of my head. I rested against him, letting my tears dampen his T-shirt, finally letting go of what I'd thought we would become. Marriage, kids, all of it gone. I thought maybe he cried too, as he held me. Neither of us spoke for the longest time. It felt a little like someone had died, and he was the only one I would want to comfort me.

When I knew I could speak without falling apart, I pulled away and wiped my nose on my sleeve. I desperately wished I had a tissue.

Carey lifted a corner of his shirt and wiped my eyes. "Please forgive me," he pleaded.

I sniffed as he mopped up the mess I'd made of my face. "I hate you," I said again, without anger.

And we both knew that I meant the opposite.

Chapter Twenty-Three

We talked for two hours after that.

I yelled at him some more. Backed into a corner, he lashed out and then apologized for lashing out. And then apologized again for lying. At one point, I actually kicked him in the shin and he swore at me. Then I asked him how he knew he was gay. I tried to put myself in his shoes, and when I did that, I could understand why he wouldn't come out. Not in our town.

We talked, but I wasn't ready to hear about the guy he had feelings for. Nor did I try to tell him about Blake. That would have snapped the tenuous hold we had on our friendship, so we danced around those topics.

After we both cried again, I tried to convince him to give me his shirt to use as a Kleenex. It was his fault I was crying, right? When he refused and handed me a leaf instead, I punched him in the ribs. I remember thinking how much I would miss him when he deployed.

Carey did not ask me to keep his secret. Not then.

That came later that night, when he showed up in my room with bruises all over his body and a bloody face. It turned out "Don't ask, don't tell" also meant "Don't get caught."

Carey broke that rule and paid for it.

Sometimes I wonder how Carey's parents would have reacted if he'd told them the truth right away. Sure, his dad acted macho. A former Marine himself, plus the owner of the only auto shop in town kind of locked that in. He put a lot of pressure on Carey, pushing him to be more, do more. His mother worked long hours, teaching history at the high school and coaching the cheer squad. Like me and my father, his family sat down to dinner every night too. Aside from the fact that both his parents attended, the shining difference was the glaring love in his house.

If they cared about you, the Breens spilled that love all over you, making you feel it right down to your toes. Carey got his ability to love wholeheartedly from his parents. But I'm not sure he trusted them to treat him with the same affection if they found out that he was gay. Part of me thinks he betrayed them, too, with his lack of trust.

It's Saturday and I'm still upset from the run-in the day before with my mother. So it completely figures that I run into Carey's mom when my father drags me to the home-and-garden center two towns over. He's determined to solve the puzzle of why his garden refuses to grow. Guilt gnaws at me. I decide to buy new bottles of weed killer and plant food to replace the ones I switched. That is, as soon as I can I abandon him in front of a table of kitchen herbs.

Mrs. Breen stands in front of a shelf of clay pots, which is right across from the Miracle-Gro. She sways slightly, her eyes staring blankly at the six-inch pots. I consider walking away, but something holds me there. This woman hugged me when I showed her my report cards. She listened to me complain about Nikki and comforted me when I fought with Angel. And when Carey and I began dating, she threatened him, telling him he'd better treat me right or he'd have her to deal with.

The very sensible thing to do would be to leave. My presence causes her pain. Everyone, especially her, has made that clear.

Yet . . . I can't do it. I can't leave her alone like this.

She doesn't move when I approach her. She doesn't even acknowledge my existence, until I call her name twice.

That blank gaze turns from plant containers to me, and I inhale. Blake was right. She's in bad shape. It takes everything I have not to hug her right then. Instead, I say her name a third time.

Finally she focuses on me. I can tell the instant it happens because she goes from blank to black in two seconds flat.

"Quinn," she says, and she sounds exhausted, like she can't even summon the energy to hate me today.

"Mrs. Breen, are you okay?"

She doesn't respond.

"Mrs. Breen, is Mr. Breen here? Or Blake?" I hope someone's there to help her.

"Why, Quinn?" Her brown eyes, so much like Carey's, pierce me. "Are you looking to break his heart too?"

For a moment, I wonder if she knows about Blake and me. If she somehow figured out we were together. That thought flicks into the wind, though, when she adds, "He's at the shop pulling an extra shift."

This is the most she's said to me in months. I take a step closer. "Have you heard anything?"

Smart, Quinn. Really smart to bring that up.

She heaves this sigh that comes from her gut. "No. No, we haven't."

"I'm sorry," I say.

If things were different, I would go to her and hold her. I could help her. I could be there for her.

She rolls her shoulders and laughs. "Well that just makes everything okay, doesn't it?"

The anger returns in her raised, acidic voice. She looks around the empty aisle. "Did you hear that, everyone? Quinn is sorry she cheated on my boy. Thank you so much. I didn't know how I was going to get through another day without your apology!"

She takes a step toward me, her entire body rippling with aggression. "Do you want to know what I think of your apologies? They're useless!"

I stand there, biting my tongue so hard I taste blood. Warm hands come to rest on my shoulders, and I nearly jump out of my skin.

"That's enough, Denise," my father says.

Carey's mom starts, and she takes a couple steps back at my father's sudden appearance.

"You have no idea what I'm going through, Cole," she answers. "Don't tell me what's enough."

Calm and sure, he does not waver. "Yelling at Quinn isn't going to make him come home."

She begins to cry, and I wish I'd never approached her. She looks like she believes he's dead. That he's never coming home.

My father tugs on me gently to steer me away. I begin to follow him, but I remember the letter. I pull away from my father to go to her.

"The week before he went missing, he wrote to me."

This gets her attention, and I continue. "He talked about sitting on my front porch and teasing me about always having to be right."

I think she's not going to answer, but she whispers, "What else did he say?"

"That he misses your cooking something fierce. MREs just aren't the same as your cooking."

She gives a tiny, husky laugh. "That sounds like Carey."

"Yeah. He asked me to tell you how much he misses you and that he loves you."

Her eyes look a little less empty than before. Again I wish I could hug her or touch her hand. But I don't dare. My father waits for me at the end of the aisle with surprise and something like sympathy on his face. I pace toward him.

If I thought Mrs. Breen would thank me, I was wrong.

But she does call my name. "Quinn."

Tears track down her stony face like rivulets of rain on a statue. "He's a hero. That's what his squadron leader says. The last they heard he was going after a rebel using a child as a shield. They didn't find him, but he helped that child get away."

I inhale a breath that turns into a smothered sob. "That sounds like Carey."

"Yeah," she whispers. Her shoulders pull back and she stands straight. "Good-bye, Quinn."

The conversation's over. I can see she's finished with me. Permanently.

My father follows me when I rush past him, holding my stomach to keep the kerosene in. One good light and I'll take down everyone around me in an explosion of truth.

At the hospital, I wait for George to wake.

He dropped off to sleep almost midsentence, something he's doing more and more frequently. I pretend it's the medication, but there's a reason he's in the long-term care ward. A reason I don't want to face.

Sitting in the chair by the window, I listen to George snore and watch the window do a pas de deux with the rain skipping over its surface. I finger the piece of paper with my mother's phone number and obsess over last week's confrontation with Carey's mom. Both women said they loved me once-upon-a-perfect-time. But they have both washed their hands of me.

At least with Carey's mom, I get it. Her anger comes from her love for her son. I'm desperately afraid for him too. I miss him so much, like half of my heart's been cut away. And suddenly, I feel a horrible sadness for Carey. He hid so much from all of us, and maybe if I'd been a better friend, he would have come out sooner. Maybe I would have had the chance to know the side of him that he kept tucked away. How can I blame him for longing to be himself? Isn't that what we all want?

"What's the matter, kid?" I look up to find George studying me from his bed. His eyes droop, but they are as sharp as ever. He adds, "You look so sad, Sophie."

I pull my legs into my chest, propping my chin on my knee. "I'm not sure how much more of this I can take," I admit.

I've told George what happened with my mother and Mrs. Breen. I could see on his face that he wished he had the solution to make all my problems go away. He doesn't know that only Carey has that ability.

"You'd be surprised what you can take. To everything there is a season. . . ."

My lips quirk into a weak smile. "You quoting scripture at me now, old man?"

He doesn't laugh like I think he will. "This pain won't last forever. You'll see."

An ache starts in my throat. "What makes you say that?"

"You're amazing, kid. You have so much to give. You have the kind of heart that can't be hidden forever. One day, people will see that about you, and you are going to knock them on their asses with how stunning you are."

I sniff and hug my legs.

We sit in silence, and he begins to drop off to sleep again.

I wait until his eyes go heavy and his breathing evens out before I tiptoe to the side of his bed and drop a kiss on his creased cheek. I turn back to my chair.

That's when George whispers, "Love you too, kid."

Chapter Twenty-Four

George decides to make a big deal of my eighteenth birthday.

I'd thought the day would pass like any other, but he rejects that notion. He arranges for a small party in the atrium, and even convinces some of the staff and patients to help him decorate the garden with lights and balloons. When I push his chair into the indoor garden, everyone yells "Surprise!" even though I saw them all through the atrium's glass. Nurse Espinoza places a silly plastic tiara on my head.

It's pretty much the best birthday ever.

I hadn't realized how many friends I'd made at the hospital in my time there. There's Don and the other soldiers I'd interviewed with George. Of course, not all of them are there. Some have transferred out, gone home, or gone back to the war front. Some have died.

Then there are the nurses and doctors I've spent time with.

George is a favorite patient, and I'm his favorite person. His friend-ships have rubbed off on me. Sitting in the midst of these people, I am so grateful to George and so glad my father made me come here to work. I wonder if he'll ever know the favor he did me.

Then, I notice George glance behind me to the atrium door. He says, "Don't be mad at me, okay?"

I laugh, still riding high on buttercream frosting. "How could I be?"

"Well . . . ," he says, looking guilty.

"Hi, Sophie," my mother says from behind me.

I shoot George a venomous glare, before turning to face her. "Hey."

She looks out of place. These are my people. Maybe they're not my age, like Ang or Nikki, but they are my friends. We are the Island of Misfit Toys, all broken or smashed in some way. She is too perfect to fit in among us, and she knows it, shift-ing her weight from one foot to the other in an uncomfortable dance. A bright purple and lime green box lies forgotten in her hand, until she pushes it toward me with a huge, nervous smile. "Happy birthday!"

When I'm silent too long, George gives my back a hearty shove. I awkwardly take the gift from her and grudgingly offer her a seat at the table with George and me. Don welcomes her and offers her a slice of cake. She takes it, steadying his shaking hands with one of hers, the warmth of her smile making him light up.

Don looks from her to me. "Are the two of you related? You must get this a lot, but you both look very alike."

If only he knew.

I snort, and George cuffs the back of my head. Rubbing my scalp, I shoot him another glare. "Do that again, and I unlock your brake at the top of a very tall hill."

He grins and shoots back, "Be nice or I'll take back my camera, brat."

I gasp. "You wouldn't!"

"Try me."

Leaving me to sulk, he tells Don, "This here is Sophie's mother. I invited her. Sophie, this old geezer is Don Baruth."

He introduces her around to my friends. If she wonders why I'm the only teenager present, she keeps it to herself. It occurs to me that my secret—this one, at least—is out. Now that folks know we are related, it's only a matter of time before my father finds out she's back. Shit.

My mother's attention bounces back and forth between me and George. I can see she's trying to figure us out. I can't blame her for that—not many people my age are best friends with old men. I wouldn't be, if not for special circumstances.

Despite her obvious discomfort at being the stranger in our midst, she greets everyone with warmth. A couple of the nurses recognize her from the third floor and ask after Uncle Eddy. She shoots me another look and changes the subject quickly, as if she thinks I'll be upset at the mention of him.

I glance at George, and I can tell he's disappointed in me. I feel the weight of it in my gut. I'm not sure how he expected me to react, inviting her here. My distress must show because he leans close and whispers, "You need someone, girl. I won't be around forever."

The happiness I'd felt before blinks out like a smashed light bulb. We don't talk about death. Not his. I can't breathe.

"Please don't say things like that. I can't—"

My lip trembles, and George's stern gaze gentles. He pats my hand. "Give her a chance, Sophie. You should've heard how happy she was when I invited her. You just might be missing out on something if you turn her away without listening to what she has to say."

I doubt it. I really do. But I can't deal with the idea of him dying. So I pretend to accept my mother's presence to make him happy.

"How is Eddy?" I ask, knowing George would approve. I don't say "Uncle." It's one thing to hear it in my head, but the word tastes like bleach on my tongue.

My mother's face lights up with affection. "Better every day. He's moved up the kidney transplant list, so things are looking up."

I can't bring myself to ask what's wrong with him. It may be harsh, but I don't care. Instead, I say, "That's good." Bland, but the best I can do.

Silence falls, and I can't think of anything else to say that won't provoke a fight. She takes charge and suggests I open my gifts.

I've already opened the ones from the staff and other patients. They'd given me a gorgeous leather case to keep George's camera in. And then I open George's gift.

I bawl like a little baby. He's given me his Nikon. Not as a loaner, but as my own. He's included a note: *Stun them all. Love, George.*

He clears his throat, and I know my reaction has touched him. I hug the camera, and he says, "No one else would take care of it like you would."

I set the camera down carefully and reach over to wrap my arms around his neck, tucking my wet face into his neck. No one has given me a gift that meant so much.

He pats my back. "Hey, now. What's this? I thought you liked it."

I laugh and sit back, wiping my face with a dessert napkin. "I love it. Honestly, George. It's the best. I promise I'll take care of it."

"You better," he threatens me with a mock glare.

I notice my mother watching us again, and I wonder what she's thinking. Pain curls into her furrowed brow and the tense way she holds herself together. She reminds me of myself at school, the odd man out. That's when I realize: It's the love. George and I so obviously care about each other, and she doesn't even know me. I know I'm right when George smacks a loud kiss on my cheek and she turns away.

I expected a moment like this to make me happy. *See how well*

I got on without you? That's what I thought would run through my mind. I didn't expect to feel sad. It's all a lie, after all. I didn't really get on so well.

George says, "Why don't you open the gift from your mother?"

I take the box and carefully pull off the wrapping paper. She twists her fingers together, wrapping them around her knee. It's a laptop. My first thought is that she's buying me off, but she sits forward and says in a rush, "It's a MacBook. George mentioned how talented you are. It has Photoshop. The computer store said it has the best software for professional photographers."

She waits nervously for my reaction. I could hurt her. That's painfully obvious. This is up to me, to choose how I will go forward with her. I decide to test the waters.

"Thank you. I love it."

I don't hug her, but she appears pleased anyway. Her knuckles lose some of their whiteness as she relaxes her grip. The conversation picks up around us as a couple of the guys break out a deck of cards. Most of the doctors and nurses return to work, but a few of us stay behind to play poker. I've learned a lot about how to play from George. My mother is better. She shocks us by raking in half the pot, while I take the other half.

George grumbles. "No fair, Sophie. You're a ringer."

"Put up or shut up," my mother and I say at the same time. Our eyes meet in surprise.

A smile breaks out across her face, and I can't help but smile back. "You remember?" she asks.

"Of course," I say. Running away to the beach was one of the best weekends of my life. We'd played cards by the pool, and when I'd gloated, she'd told me that adults could never beat a kid at Go Fish. "Go Fish is in my blood."

That's what I'd bragged six years ago. She laughs at the memory, and it hurts to see it. She's beautiful. Much more so than I remembered. Age has changed her, but there's a generosity to her features that I don't recall. Then again, maybe I was too young to notice. The changes in her are like music missing the refrain. The song's transformed, though what's left remains familiar.

George squeezes my hand, and I squeeze back.

He's right, in a way. I can't run from her. The pain she caused won't disappear if I stick my fingers in my ears and shut my eyes like a two-year-old throwing a tantrum.

George looks tired, and I think it's time I got him back to his room. We wrap up the poker game, and I leap into the unknown, asking my mother, "Do you have time to grab a coffee?"

Before she can answer, her eyes round in a combination of shock and fear.

"What the hell are you doing here, Sophie?" my father asks.

Chapter Twenty-Five

Now I know why soldiers make a habit of always sitting with their back to the wall. That way you can't be surprised by a bomb exploding behind you.

My father's as furious as the day he returned home to find she'd left with his brother. His shoulders look broader, more muscled than ever. The fear in my mother's expression makes sense, even though I know he would never hurt her. He's too controlled for that.

I'm tempted to jump up between them, but George stays me with a hand on my arm and a swift shake of his head. I jut my chin forward. *Did you invite him here?* He shakes his head again. He had nothing to do with this.

I wonder how my father found out she was at the hospital. Then I notice the gift bag in his hand. Someone told him they were having a party for me today, and he came by to bring his gift.

My mother—never the coward—rises from her chair. "Cole."

He ignores her greeting and asks again, "What are you doing here?"

"She's my daughter. I have every right to be here."

He snorts. "You gave that right up when you walked out and never looked back."

"Do you really want to go there?" she challenges him.

Her dark tone makes him pause. A look flashes between them that I don't understand.

She continues. "I'm done, Cole. I won't stay away anymore. As long as Sophie wants me here, I'm not going anywhere."

"Quinn," he says, with a triumphant look. "She goes by Quinn now."

His words hurt her. Worse, they hurt me. Everyone who's stayed behind to play cards watches them argue, and I'm humiliated. My parents talk about me as if I'm not there. As if my opinion doesn't matter.

George has had enough. He pushes his chair back from the table. "This is a celebration for your daughter's birthday. Don't you think you ought to talk about this privately?"

My father shifts his icy gaze to George. "Don't tell me how to deal with my family. When I sent Quinn here, it was to keep her from getting into any more trouble. Bang-up job you've done with her, encouraging her to see her mother behind my back."

I squeeze the armrests of my chair and grit my teeth. I won't cry in front of all these people. Not even when my father reveals how much he hates me in front of everyone.

"Why, you couldn't see who she is if you—"

George's furious words are cut short by a hacking cough that sounds like it's ripping his lungs apart. He collapses back in his chair, blood on his white lips, and my father rushes to yell for a nurse in the hall. It takes all of thirty seconds for the nurses to rush in, assess him, and push us out of the garden.

Everything spins when I'm standing in the hallway. Another few minutes and George rolls out of the atrium on a gurney, and I can't tell if he's asleep or unconscious. I touch George's shoulder, and he shoots me a tired smile before they take him away.

My parents have been reunited for five minutes and already they've managed to destroy my world again.

Please, please be okay, George.

Why do I always come in last place for these two?

Things weren't much different the last time I saw my parents together. I was ten, and my father was home on a six-week leave. Iraq had left its mark on him. Even as a kid, I could see that. Later I learned that my father had been in the thick of the first Iraq invasion. As Carey put it, my father must have seen some scary shit. My father didn't talk about it, though. Not to me. Not to anyone, I suspected.

Instead, he brooded. A lot. And when he wasn't brooding, he

watched us, my mother and me, as if we were foreign invaders in his home. I tiptoed around him, but my mother smashed into him head-on.

They fought all the time: He didn't give us enough attention. She demanded too much. He didn't understand how hard it was for her to raise a kid alone. She had no idea what he'd gone through over there, and she didn't appreciate how he was doing it for me. On and on, they circled each other, trading accusations for insults.

I ran away to Carey's whenever I could. When that wasn't possible, I hid in my room and wondered if it would be easier for them if I wasn't part of the equation.

One fight in particular left bruises. They'd been at it all day, neither of them backing down. I sat against my bedroom door, eavesdropping. They said the same things they always did, but this time my mother asked him a question that changed the tone of the conversation.

"Cole, before we got married, you promised that our family would come first. When are you going to make good on that?"

After a long silence, he said, "You're asking the impossible. I have responsibilities. My men—"

"It's not your men I'm worried about!" Her voice gentled and I had to put my ear against the wood to hear her. "It's Sophie. You're missing out on everything. Why can't you see that?"

My father sounded brittle. "You think I don't see how much I've missed? Her first steps, her first words, her first day at school.

When I'm over there, I think about it all the time. Geez, Sophie, it ripped me up when I missed her birth!"

"I know, Cole. But at some point, there won't be any more firsts for you to miss out on."

"You expect me to just walk out? Men are dying over there."

"And I'm dying over here!"

The argument veered back into regular territory with him accusing her of being overly dramatic and her telling him to fuck off. I'd heard enough, and packed a bag to spend the night at Carey's. I decided to risk my parents being upset and leave without their permission. Mrs. Breen could call them later. They probably wouldn't notice anyway.

As I tiptoed down the hall to the front door, the shouting grew louder. Before I closed the door behind me, I overheard my father say one thing I would never forget. He told my mother that he hated who she'd become. And he added, "And you're making Sophie just like you."

Some words hit you like a tree branch slapping you in the face. And some words rip into your flesh, leaving scars so deep, they never completely fade.

"Sophie," my mother says to my back as I watch George disappear down the hall. "I'm so sorry. I'm sure he's going to be okay."

"No," I tell her. "He's not. He's dying." My quiet words sound like bullets. I turn to my parents. They stand a few feet apart, but they might as well be standing on the opposite shores of a river. "Why did you come here? This was the one good thing I had left. Why did you have to ruin it?"

My father speaks up. "Quinn—"

"Stop calling her that!" my mother says.

He turns, ready to lay into her, and I shout, "Shut up! Just once, could the two of you stop thinking about yourselves?"

I stride up to my mother. "Mom, you left. Dad stayed. You don't know me, and you don't have any rights where I'm concerned."

She winces, but I am already turning on my father. He looks cold and distant, and my throat aches when my breath catches on a sob. "Dad, I'm not Mom. She left. Stop blaming me for what she did to you."

His face drains of color. I fall back several steps, really crying now.

"I'm standing right in front of you, and you can't even see me!"

The only people who see me aren't here. Carey may be dead, and George comes closer to death every day.

I can't breathe. My parents steal the air with their hatred. I run away, hitting the door to the stairs at a jog.

The last thing I hear is them calling my name.

Mom: "Sophie!"

Dad: "Quinn!"

Me:

Chapter Twenty-Six

Grave Woods has become my third home after the hospital and my house. That's where I go when I leave the VA. Now that it's mid-May, you can feel summer around the corner. It's chilly tonight, but I can't feel it anymore. Hours ago, I called the hospital to check on George. He was doing okay on oxygen, they told me, but they wouldn't let me in to see him again today. He needed rest.

I've cried until I've turned myself inside out.

I roll onto my side on Josephine's grave, the hard ground biting into my hip. George is my rock. What will I do without him? I knew he wasn't doing well, but I turned away from it. What kind of friend am I?

I've spent enough time at the hospital to understand what's coming next.

I don't know if I can watch it happen. I'm not brave enough

to watch him fade. Maybe if I hadn't covered for Carey, I would be stronger.

But then, was that choice any easier?

The day after I spoke with Carey in Grave Woods, I realized our conversation hadn't really solved anything. Not how I felt about Carey's confession or about my feelings for Blake. I wasn't sure how I felt about sleeping with him, or if I should tell Carey about it. What would I say?

Sweating in the summer heat, I lay on my bed, imagining how Carey would react and hoping a cooling breeze would blow through the open window. Every memory of Carey was colored by my new knowledge of him: The things he'd said. The promises he'd made. And the lies he'd told to keep his secret. I got angry every time I thought about it. Despite his sweet words, I wondered if our friendship was worth saving. How could I forgive him?

I spent hours stuck in that loop, like a hamster on a wheel—working but never getting any closer to an answer.

Then Carey climbed through my window and dropped to the floor. He didn't drop so much as he collapsed in a heap on the floor. Shocked, I tossed away the pillow I'd been hugging and sat up.

"Carey?"

He didn't answer, but he lay there gasping with an arm draped over his face. I scooted off the bed and crawled toward him. When I reached for his elbow he rolled toward me, and I inhaled when I saw the blood. At first glance, he was covered in it. His face, his shirt, his hair.

I tried to stand, and he tugged on my hand.

"No! Don't tell anyone!"

I understood he meant my father. "He's not here. I need the first-aid kit. I'll be right back."

He let me go and I ran through my house, skidding through the hall in my slippers before I kicked them off. In seconds I was back, ripping the lid off the white plastic case.

"What happened, Carey?"

My voice sounded oddly calm, as I went about mopping up the blood with a wet towel I'd brought with me.

He winced. "My fault. I knew better." He groaned when I pulled off his shirt.

With few words, he told me how he'd gone to meet a friend at Joe's, a bar two towns over with a reputation for looking the other way when carding underage Marines. He'd gone to meet Ben.

Ben, I thought. Finally, *he* had a name. The guy Carey had fallen for.

Carey had tried to end it, believing their relationship had no future. Not with them both about to be deployed. Not when they could both get discharged if they were caught. Ben had kissed him in the parking lot. A good-bye kiss before he drove away.

Except they hadn't been alone. Several Marines saw the whole thing. They'd beat the shit out of Carey and left him bleeding in the parking lot. They'd said they didn't want a fag in their battalion. He might put the moves on them over there, and they didn't want a homo sneaking onto their cots at night.

I listened to all of this, and I wanted to hit Carey. I wanted to throw up. I wanted to scratch my nails down his face and call him a thousand names. Instead, I yanked my hands back the second I'd taped the last bandage, not wanting to touch him.

When he finished speaking, I packed up the first-aid kit, setting aside the used bandages for the trash. A raised welt darkened Carey's left cheekbone, the skin alternating shades of pink and red that would later turn blue and purple. A cut hid just below his hairline. Judging from the glass I'd pulled out of it with tweezers, someone had smashed a bottle over his head.

The room grew eerily quiet as we stared at each other. If he was outted, his career was over.

"Quinn?" he asked, sounding uncertain and scared.

"I don't want to hear any more about him." I couldn't even say his name—Ben's name—out loud. "Why the hell would you come here? Why didn't you go to Ben if he's the one you love?"

I sounded like my father, cold rage vibrating in my voice.

"I didn't think." He tried to sit up, managing only to get as far as turning to lean against the wall. "You're my best friend."

I deflated beside him. He reached for my hand, and his palm rubbed rough and familiar against mine. He dipped his head to press his lips to my fingers. A tender gesture, but one without passion. For a moment I wished everything could be like it had been. Uncomplicated. Simple. Expected. But we'd gone too far. Done things we couldn't take back.

"I don't know what to do, Quinn. Please help me. I've fucked everything up. Tell me what to do. I need you."

He started sobbing, his shoulders shaking. My cold heart cracked. He'd held me every time I ran to him. No questions. No judgments. Just solace and friendship and warmth. I wrapped an arm around him and he twisted, falling into my lap.

My entire life, no one had ever said they needed me. My parents certainly didn't need me. Blake? Maybe he wanted me, but he didn't need me. As I held Carey, I had only one choice. At least, only one choice I could live with.

"We'll figure something out. I promise."

I didn't know how I'd regret those words.

The next day, we drove one town over to attend our football team's summer scrimmage. We arrived as a couple, with Carey's arm looped over my shoulders. We joked about his bruises, saying he'd fallen while we were hiking, too caught up in me to notice where he was going. Nobody questioned the excuse or doubted we were together. Not even Blake, who looked like I'd plunged a knife into his stomach. The first chance he had, he pulled me away from Carey and cornered me under the bleachers.

"What's going on, Q?"

"Nothing," I answered defensively. I didn't know how else to deal with him, except to shut him out. To make him think I was a bitch. I'd already promised Carey I wouldn't out him to anyone, that I'd protect his secret at all costs. Of course, I couldn't have guessed what that cost would be.

"You're together," he said in a flat voice.

"Yes," I said, and he gave me such a look of hatred, I took two steps back. That seemed to push him into action, and he came at me. I expected anger, but his arms were gentle as he pulled me toward him.

"You care about me," he said. "You couldn't kiss me the way you did and not care about me."

I'd prepared myself for this. I shook my head. "I'm sorry. You saw what you wanted to."

"You're lying," he said. A new determination in his voice. "I'll prove it."

He kissed me then. More than anger, I felt desperation from him. And the longer he held me—his lips tugging at mine, trying to convince me that he was the one—the harder it became to argue.

Blake cared about me. Deeply. And I felt the same about him. I threw myself into his embrace, and suddenly it became more. Clothes shifting, the warm evening air hitting my skin, and then his skin against my skin.

A roar went up from the crowd as somebody scored a touchdown.

Crashing back to reality, I stumbled away from Blake, yanking my clothes back on. Our gazes met: his hopeless and mine apologizing. His eyes seared me before I ran. Maybe we would have tried to pretend it never happened, that we never happened.

A week later Jamie posted that picture of us on Facebook, and the possibility of Blake and me staying friends was shot to hell.

A branch snaps, and I wake in a rush. It is pitch-black, and I am in Grave Woods. Not the smartest idea, since it appears I'm no longer alone. Animal or human? I tilt my head to listen. Footsteps are coming toward me.

A flashlight soars through the clearing, lighting up the trees before it lands on me, still lying on the ground. Then he steps into view. Blake.

"Q! There you are!" He rushes toward me, dropping to his knees. For once, he's dressed for the weather, in a jacket and flannel shirt. "Are you okay? Shit, you had me scared!"

"What are you doing here?" I ask, confused.

"Your dad called, asking if I'd seen you. He said you ran off from the hospital."

My parents arguing. George. The day rushes back to me, and I fight Blake's attempt to get me to my feet by wrapping my arms around my knees. I'm not ready to go back and face them.

"Come on, Q," he says when I refuse to get up. "Your skin is like ice. We have to get you to your Jeep."

"Go away, Blake."

He doesn't. He sits beside me, dropping the flashlight on the ground between us. "What the fuck is going on? Your dad sounds freaked out, and you're out here in the woods in the middle of the night."

He sounds strained, and I concentrate on his voice.

"He found out that my mom's back."

"Oh man. Wait—if he just found out, how long have you known?"

"Since before the dance," I admit.

"Aw, Q," he groans. "Why didn't you tell me?"

I start crying. "Why would I? We're not friends anymore."

He loops an arm around my shoulder, tugging me into the side of his body. My skin soaks up the heat coming off him. He sighs. "We're more than friends. That's kind of the problem, isn't it?" He runs a hand over my back, trying to warm me up. "I'm here now. Talk to me."

I do. He flips off the flashlight to save the battery, and in the dark I tell him about my mom's return and my friendship with George and how my father's treated me since the picture came out. I tell him about my run-ins with Jamie and Nikki and Angel and Mrs. Breen. I confess how dirty I've felt—the kind that stains you below the skin. Except everyone can see these stains, and they have punished me for them.

I tell him how shitty the past months have been, and how I felt abandoned by everyone, including Carey. Including him.

Blake listens to me unload in silence, much like I listened to Carey that night he crawled through my window. I stop just short of confessing the part where Carey is gay and I promised him I would pretend I was still his girlfriend to save him. I keep my promise, but just.

At some point, he lies back in the dirt, and I curl into his body while he holds tight to me. When my teeth begin to chatter, Blake strips off his coat and drapes it over us. My throat hurts from talking by the time I run out of words.

We listen to crickets chirping, and he says, "I'm sorry. For everything that's happened to you. I'm so sorry."

He doesn't lie and say he didn't know it was happening. Some of it he witnessed; some of it I kept from him deliberately. I'd owed him that for hurting him. But Blake also was my friend. More than a friend, like he said. He'd owed me something too.

I roll my head against his shoulder so I can see his face. "I'm sorry too."

"Happy birthday, Q," he whispers.

He dips his head toward me, and I meet him halfway. Lips touch, tug, part. *I love him,* I think, my lips curving into a small smile at the certainty. No more confusion. His fingers trace my cheek, tucking my hair behind my ear in a gentle movement that sets off shivers.

I wrap my hand around the back of his neck. *I love him,* I think again.

He pulls away an inch, and we inhale one breath. His hand

drops to my waist. When I kiss him, he grips my shirt, resting his fist on my hip.

"I love you, Q," he whispers. "I always have, even when you were Carey's."

I roll onto my back and he follows, dropping tiny kisses on my neck. Leaning over me, he waits for me to open my eyes. "Don't break my heart again, okay?"

"I promise," I whisper back.

And then we stop talking.

Chapter Twenty-Seven

The porch light is on when I get home, even though the sun peeks over the horizon. Blake waves from his truck, waiting until I'm inside before he pulls away. I fall back against the front door for a moment, too unsteady to stand without support.

Everything can change in a heartbeat.

I'm in love with a boy who loves me back.

I walk down the hall to peer into the living room. The TV drones on, tuned to an early a.m. infomercial. My father sits on the couch, his arms crossed and his chin dropped on his chest as he sleeps. Blake had called him hours before to say he'd bring me home when I was ready. He'd insisted, so a search party wasn't sent out for us. My father hadn't even argued.

I leave him sleeping.

After showering, I put on my pajamas and head for my room. My gifts from my birthday party have been piled on my dresser, including the laptop from my mother. A gift bag sits on my bed—the one my father had brought to the hospital—and I open it. He must have talked to George, too. He bought me an expensive tripod to go with George's camera.

"Do you like it?"

My father stands in the doorway, leaning against the jamb. I can't read his expression. He's not cold, but he's not giving much away, either.

I glance at the package in my lap and nod. "Very much. It's perfect. George told you he was giving me the Nikon?"

His forehead wrinkles in confusion. "That camera was George's? I thought it was yours."

"You didn't talk to him?" I ask, surprised.

He shakes his head slowly. "No. You never go anywhere without that thing. I thought maybe the tripod would come in handy."

"It will," I say.

Last year he'd given me tickets to an amusement park. I hadn't been to one since I was little, and I'd never used them, and eventually I gave them away. But he'd put thought into this gift. My father had noticed something I loved.

"I see you," he says, as if he's read my thoughts.

Maybe sometimes. It's a start. I can give something in return.

"Dad, you know how I applied to Boston University's photojournalism program? I got accepted."

He only looks surprised for a second before he pulls me off the bed to give me a bear hug. "I'm so proud of you, sweetheart."

And he is proud. It's all over him, and I wonder why I waited so long to tell him or anyone else.

"Thanks, Dad."

"How about we celebrate tomorrow? I'll take you out to dinner."

"What about Mom?" I ask.

He lets me go. "Quinn, we need to talk. Maybe after we both get some sleep."

"I think we need to talk now," I argue, crossing my arms.

He shoots me a warning look. "Don't push it. You stayed out all night without calling, and I'm trying to cut you some slack here. Like I said, let's get some rest."

I watch him walk away from me. I should let him go. My emotions are spinning all over the place. That's exactly why I can't let him go.

"I'm not a kid anymore. You can't just tell me to obey." I raise my voice. "You said she was never coming back. I was eleven and my heart was broken and I wanted you to tell me she still loved me. Do you remember that? You told me she was gone and I needed to grow up and stop wishing she'd come back."

He glances over his shoulder. "You said it yourself. You're not a kid anymore, Quinn. Adults make mistakes. I'm sorry I disappointed you, but I've done the best I could."

He leaves, closing my door behind him.

I shout, "You should've tried harder!"

Footsteps pause in the hall, and then fade as he walks away.

*　*　*

It's a school day, but I decide to skip. I think I've earned it after the night before. I sleep the morning away and wake to an empty house. My father's left a note. *Quinn—Fixings for veggie omelets in the fridge. I'll be home late. Dad.* A man of few words.

His idea of an apology?

After eating and dressing, I head to the hospital. George is asleep, and I drop my purse and camera bag on the floor and settle in. Oxygen tubes run into his nose, and he's hooked to an IV for the first time I can remember in a long time. His skin appears thin, as if the slightest scratch could puncture it. The signs have been there all along. I've just been ignoring them.

His eyes open, and for a moment he looks lost. I step toward the bed, and he focuses on me. Then he says, "I'm not dead yet. Stop looking at me like that or you can get the hell out of here."

I squeeze his hand. "Shut up, old man. You scared the crap out of me yesterday. The least you can do is put up with a few tears."

"Not a chance," he says, but he squeezes my hand. He gestures to his table, and I pour him a cup of water from a plastic pitcher. He's more worn-out than he's letting on, because he lets me tip the straw to his lips while he drinks. He frowns. "Not much of a birthday yesterday, was it?"

I pull my chair closer so I can hook my legs on the rail of his bed. "The best-laid plans . . ."

"What happened?"

He grills me on everything that unfolded after he collapsed. I blush when I get to the part about Blake finding me in the woods, even though I leave out most of the details. I don't fool George.

"So it's like that, is it?" He chortles when I suddenly find the wall behind him fascinating. "You're in love with this boy. Blake."

He doesn't sound judgmental. In fact, he doesn't even sound surprised.

"You knew," I accuse.

"I guessed. Something in your voice whenever you mention him. How you mostly avoid talking about him. He the boy in the picture?"

I say nothing, giving him an obstinate look.

"Geez, you're a mule. Keep your secret then."

"Are you mad?" I ask.

He smiles. "Nah. Whatever you are, you're honorable, kid. If you won't talk, you have your reasons. Mysterious and screwed up as they might be."

I shoot him a relieved smile. "Quit being mean to me or I won't tell you my news."

"There's more? I'm not sure I can take it."

I tell him about Boston University, and he lets out with a whoop that sets off a spate of coughing. A nurse I don't know pops his head in to check on us, and as soon as George has breath, he tells the nurse the news. He's like a proud papa. A warm glow settles over me, one I didn't feel even when I shared the news with my father.

It hits me.

George won't be alive to see me graduate college. Maybe not even high school.

The amused nurse wanders off, and George notices how quiet I am.

"You've finally figured it out, haven't you?" he says.

"How long, George?"

For once, he doesn't put on a brave face. I need an answer, and he understands that.

"The docs say a few weeks if I'm lucky. Things are happening fast now, kid."

I clamp my jaw tight. George hasn't asked much of me. Honesty and friendship. I can avoid the tears and the whole maudlin scene for him.

"Well, that's a pisser." I inject as much humor in my voice as I can, but my words fall flat.

He attempts to sit up, and I jump up to help him, shoving pillows behind his back. "I'm being serious," he says when I back away. "I think maybe you shouldn't keep coming here. I don't want you to see this."

I fall back on my heels. *He's trying to send me away. For my own good.* That's the only thing that enables me to rein in my anger.

"Fuck you," I say. He glares, but I cut him off before he can speak. "Listen up, old man. I've put up with a lot of shit this year. I'm not going to take any from you. And I'm not leaving. I thought you knew me better than that."

"This isn't about being a good friend—"

"No, you're right." I busy myself, tucking his blanket around him. "It's about family. You're my family, stupid."

George's eyes well up, and I look away. It sounds cheesy, but it's the freaking truth: I love the old guy.

I clear my throat. "Can we agree not to talk about this again?"

He huffs. "Are you kidding? I'm about to go into diabetic shock from all the sweetness."

"You're not diabetic, George."

"Exactly."

We change the subject. He asks, "Did you bring your camera?"

My camera, I think, and glow at the thought. I nod, and he says, "Get my tape recorder out of my dresser, will you?"

The Veterans History Project is the last thing I want to think about today, but I do as he asks. "You're not thinking of doing any interviews today, are you? You need to rest."

He pushes the recorder into my hand when I try to give it to him. "There's one interview we haven't done," he says.

He stares me down, challenging me to turn away. I don't get it at first. And then I realize.

We've never collected George's story.

He doesn't pressure me. Doesn't remind me that time's winding away from us. He gives me a chance to refuse. But it's too late for that. I'd already decided to stay.

So I turn all business, having watched him do this dozens of times. I grab my camera. I set up the recorder on his rolling tray table. When everything is ready, I hit record and begin speaking.

> "Today is May fifteenth and I am interviewing George Wilkins at the Fayetteville Veterans Hospital. My name is Sophie Topper Quinn and I'll be the interviewer. George, could you state for the recording what war and branch of service you served in?"

Chapter Twenty-Eight

School is an afterthought. It's the blockade standing between visiting the hospital and a future away from Sweethaven. The only thing I'm looking forward to at school is seeing Blake again. We haven't talked since he followed me home from Grave Woods. It's more my fault than his, since I took a few days off of school to spend time with George. I've tried calling him, but he hasn't called back.

Walking on Sweethaven High's campus, I feel like a ghost, existing between two planes of reality. I don't belong here anymore. It's at once bittersweet and triumphant. Somehow I miss seeing Blake all day. Then it's time for Yearbook.

Today's the last day to turn in photos. Most everything has already been submitted, but Mr. Horowitz begged the printer for a deadline extension in order to get my pictures in. He takes the flash drive from me and plugs it into his computer. Rubbing his hands together with glee, he begins the process of clicking through the hundreds of photos I've taken these last weeks. A group of students crowd around his oversized monitor to see them over his shoulder.

The dance. The shots from DC. Static team photos. My favorites are the ones I took on my own without an assignment. The weeks everyone pretended to ignore me had led to some great images. A couple kissing. A shot of another couple's hands. A senior basketball player showing a freshman how to do a layup during gym.

A sophomore I don't know that well gives me a look of respect. "These are really good."

Then Jamie says, wrinkling her nose, "What's that supposed to be?"

For some reason—maybe a desire to prove I'd survived this year despite her best efforts—I've included photos of the damage to my locker. A shot of Jamie sneering as she said something awful about me to Nikki and Angel. One of Josh looking menacing as he watched me when he thought I didn't notice. And a collage of all the comments people had made about me on Facebook and elsewhere with the picture of me and the faceless Blake in the center. My mom was right. Photoshop was handy.

An uncomfortable silence falls over the room. I'd taken these pictures without ever planning to show them to anyone. George had taught me to always have my camera ready, then let my instincts take over. My instincts had made a record of what happened to me—the good and the bad.

"We should delete those," Jamie says, reaching for the mouse. "I told you she was a wreck."

Mr. Horowitz politely but firmly intervenes. "Miss Winterburn, I asked Miss Quinn to share *all* her photos. Not just the pretty ones she thought we'd print."

Jamie's jaw drops, and I realize my own mouth has fallen open too. I try to hide a small smile, but I can't help it. I'm savoring this moment.

Mr. Horowitz leaves up the collage, and then turns his heavy gaze on my classmates. They shift and fidget to varying degrees, and he lingers longest on Jamie. "What don't you like about these pictures, Miss Winterburn? Is it because they don't show us as the best version of ourselves?"

Frustration colors her cheeks a brilliant red, and Jamie looks away, refusing to answer. Mr. Horowitz finally closes out the screen and rises. I'm about to go back to my desk when he holds a hand out to me.

"Miss Quinn, you once said that I didn't know you. I'm very sorry for that."

I give an unsteady nod and shake his hand.

He smiles and adds, "Please tell me you're going to do something with all this talent. I'm going to be sick if you tell me you're planning to be an accountant."

I smile back. "I got accepted into Boston University's photo-journalism program."

"Ah! War correspondent?" he guesses, his brows disappearing into his curly mane.

I nod, pleased he remembered our conversation on the bus and my passion for telling the stories of our soldiers.

"Congratulations. I see great things in your future."

Mr. Horowitz claps his hands, bringing the moment to an end. He whips our class back into action, dividing everyone into teams to go through the photos and decide which ones should go where.

After class, I rush out, intending to find Blake.

Jamie's voice stops me. "You don't deserve it."

I spin to face her. Everything about her is brittle and cruel. I don't ask what she means, but she continues anyway.

"To profit from what you did to Carey. You don't deserve it. Not that college or the attention."

On our field trip, Blake told me that I egged her on. He's right. She pushes, and I push back. I don't need to do that anymore. Jamie doesn't matter. With everything she has going for her, she's loved a boy who would never love her back. Maybe she's moved on now with Jimmy Manning, the boy she kissed on the bus. Then again, she's always loved Carey, even when she dated others. Jamie's stuck in this ghost world, and I'm busting out.

I smile, and she looks wary. I think, *Just try to stop me from taking what I want.*

In the end, all I say is "Good-bye, Jamie," before leaving her behind.

I find Blake at the auto shop.

He's lying on his back on a dolly with only his feet visible like the Ford 4Runner's eating him alive. After a quick glance around for Mr. Breen, I bend down to tug on his leg to get his attention. A thud followed by a curse bursts from under the hood.

I almost giggle, but the glare on his face when he rolls out the dolly stops me.

"Q, you scared the shit out of me. I thought I was alone."

"Sorry."

He sits up, rubbing his head, and I watch him, trying to gauge his mood.

"Hey," I say.

"Hey."

Blake stands and walks over to the counter against the wall that's covered with tools. He picks up a dirty rag, wiping grease from his fingers. I'm at a loss. When he left me Monday morning, everything was good between us. More than good.

"Everything okay?" I ask hesitantly. "You seem upset."

"I'm fine," he says, but he doesn't sound believable.

When I called and left messages during the past few days, I

thought maybe he was too busy with the Breens and work to call back. Maybe I'd been too caught up with George to notice when he didn't return my messages. Now it occurs to me that I should have paid more attention.

"What's going on, Blake?"

He sighs. "Nothing, Q. I told you. I'm just busy. I have two more cars to look at after this truck, and I'm a little short-handed."

I try again. "So, let me help. Tell me what to do."

"And if Mr. Breen shows up?" he asks. "Listen, I have a lot to do. I'll call you later."

"Wow." I stand, shoving my hands into my pockets so I won't hit him. He sounds dismissive, as if I'm some girl making an unwanted pass. "What the hell is wrong with you?"

"What did you expect?" he says belligerently. "I work here. This is the Breens' shop. Did you think we'd kiss and hug and be the perfect couple?"

That hurts. It stings like a bitch, actually. He's trying to pick a fight with me, and I don't understand why. I refuse to bite. "You said you loved me. I guess I expected that hadn't changed since Sunday."

The anger fades as suddenly as it flared.

"Look," I say, holding out my hands palms-up, "you don't want me here, I'm gone. But don't screw with me. Be a man, Blake."

He rubs a hand over his face, leaving behind a smudge

of grease. "I do love you, Q. I swear it. But how can we be together? Nothing's really changed, has it? We both have promises to keep."

My eyes water. Two steps forward, eight steps back into the hole I've been trying to crawl out of. He sees my expression and starts toward me, but I wave him off. I don't want to be touched. I'll fall apart completely if he touches me.

"No. You're right. I mean, it's not like we had a chance anyway, right? " I try to smile, pretending for all I'm worth that I'm not crying, too. "I'll see you around, okay?"

A phone rings from the counter, and Blake picks it up, snarling a hello. It's the Breens. I can see it in his tight, guilty expression and the way he gives me his shoulder.

He tells them, "Sure. I'll close up right now. Is that Mrs. Breen crying?"

A pause while he listens. The color drains from his face. I've never seen Blake look so scared. "What did they say?" Another pause and he's scrambling for the TV remote on the counter. "What channel?" he says as he flicks on the shop's old beater TV.

He lands on whatever channel Mr. Breen tells him. A reporter stands in front an unknown village in a nondescript desert. She's shouting to be heard over the background chaos of distant RPGs and gunfire.

"Initial reports say the Marines have located Lance Corporal

Carey Breen of the 1/6 Battalion. Breen went missing back in February when his unit was taking heavy fire during a patrol in Marjah. With no hostage demands, many had suspected he was a POW of local Taliban forces. Breen's condition is unknown at this time, but we do know he's suffered from multiple gunshot wounds. . . ."

I don't hear any more. The picture switches to the green-black night-vision camera, and there's Carey. I grab for support and find Blake. I walk into his arms without another thought. He holds me so tight I can't breathe, and we stare at the TV, devouring the first sighting we've had in months of our best friend.

Several Marines bear Carey on a gurney and another holds an IV in the air. He's strapped down and most of him is covered, except for his face. He's lost weight like he hasn't eaten in ages. His eyes are closed and he's unmoving.

"He looks dead," I whisper.

Blake hushes me. "He could be sleeping. We don't know."

The shot switches back to the reporter who doesn't seem to know anything else.

"Nobody. Just a customer," Blake says into the phone I forgot he was holding, obviously not wanting to explain why I was at the shop. "What are they telling you?"

The Marines would have sent a liaison to their home to preempt the news reports. My father had acted as that liaison before, calling upon a local Marine's family to let them know their son or daughter wasn't coming home.

Blake listens for a moment. "I'll be there as soon as I can," he says, and hangs up.

"What did they say?" I ask, desperate.

"Not much." He sets me aside and tears about the shop, grabbing his jacket, rolling the large doors closed, and shutting off machines and lights as he goes. "They're flying him to the hospital in Landstuhl. The Breens are hopping a flight to Germany and will meet him there."

At the front door, he finally notices I'm not behind him. "Q, I'm sorry," he pleads. "I have to go now. They need me. I swear I'll call you the second I hear anything."

The panic in his voice releases my feet from the floor. I follow him out and watch him run for his truck. His tires burn rubber as he peels out of the parking lot without a backward glance. My legs feel like they might give out as I climb into my Jeep.

I see Carey's face again.

He's alive.

A thousand prayers are answered.

He's alive.

My phone rings, and I answer without checking the caller ID. My father says, "Quinn?"

I start crying. "Dad, did you hear? They found Carey. He's alive!"

"I heard. Baby, listen . . ." Something's off in his voice. The happiness that should be there isn't. "You had a message here at the house from the hospital."

No, no, NO.

"It's George."

Chapter Twenty-Nine

Day one: George is on a ventilator.

Mostly he sleeps. He looks weak and helpless, not like George at all.

I read to him. I talk to him.

And I tell him about Carey. About growing up with Carey and loving Carey and believing I'd still know Carey when I'm eighty. And I confess how worried I am because nobody will tell me how Carey's doing since he was found, and the news is full of fluff and speculation and short on real reporting.

What I know:

A) Carey is alive.

B) George is dying.

C) Life just isn't fucking fair.

Negative to balance the positive. Salt with the sugar.

Sometimes I'm not sure if George can even hear me. I wonder

if it would be okay to tell him Carey's secret, but I don't. George would understand that I'm leaving that confession to Carey, now that he's been found.

When I'm sure George is sleeping, I work on his entry for the Library of Congress. Anything to keep busy while my head spins in circles about everything I don't know. George wants me to finish this, and I won't let him down. Surprisingly, even after all this time, he has few photos among his belongings at the hospital. Those I've seen him with were from other patients. He's spent hours sorting and organizing them so people wouldn't forget what these men and women have sacrificed.

Who will remember what George has done?

Day two: Blake stops by.

He stands in the doorway, shuffling his feet, while he updates me on Carey's status in Landstuhl. Three surgeries in a matter of days. He'd taken two bullets—one to the chest and one to the leg. Without proper treatment, he'd picked up an infection. Things are "touch-and-go." More doctor-speak for he may still die, and don't get your hopes up.

Blake tells me all this, the whole time standing as close to the door as he can be without leaving the room. I wonder if it's George's impending death, the steady beeps of his heart monitor, and eau de antiseptic that bothers him so much. Or maybe he still thinks I hold out hope for us, now that Carey is back.

I just don't have the energy to care.

When Blake leaves, I glance up to find George watching me, fully aware. Who knows how much he's heard, but it's enough. Unable to speak around the tube in his throat, he raises his brows. *That Blake?*

"Yeah. That's Blake."

He waggles his brows at me, and I laugh a little, shaking my head.

"I know, right? They don't make 'em like that anymore."

He points at his own chest and scowls.

I roll my eyes. "Quit fishing for compliments." He smiles, and I take my seat with my feet on the bed where his leg should be. "Did you hear what he said? About Carey?"

He nods and makes a gesture like holding a phone to his ear.

"No. Nobody's called."

He scowls.

"It's okay. I didn't expect them to. Honest." It's the truth, though that doesn't mean I'm not disappointed. After all the years Carey and I were friends, the Breens haven't dropped me so much as a text. If not for Blake, I would be getting my news about my best friend from CNN.

I change the subject because George and I have an unspoken contract to avoid sappy, maudlin topics. When he's awake, like now, we keep things light. Nurse Espinoza dropped off some flowers for him a few hours ago, and I make a big deal of this, trying to make him blush. He looks caught between telling a dirty joke and wanting to chuckle. The tube prevents either.

Eventually he drops off to sleep, and I'm left staring out the window at the black night. I don't even know what time it is.

My body sinks into the chair, weighted by misery.

Day three: More of the same.

The doctors remove the ventilator at George's request.

He tries to convince me to go home in a series of grunts and rude gestures. He's decided he doesn't want me to see him like this. Not by myself.

I hold his hand. That's what we do when things are bad.

He sleeps. A wise man, he knows when it's time to give up on an argument.

Day four: Mom shows up after I've eaten a cafeteria dinner of limp lettuce someone thought would make a good salad.

She doesn't knock, but pokes her head through the open doorway. When she sees George sleeping, she tiptoes in and whispers, "I thought you might want some company."

My eyes well up.

This isn't about me, but fuck, none of it has been. She's the first one to offer a little kindness, though, and I scrub my face to hide the effect that small gesture has on me.

I point to the free chair, and she moves it closer to mine. We speak in hushed tones by the light of the muted TV.

"How's he doing?"

I shake my head, biting my lip. She reaches over to squeeze my hand.

"I'm sorry," she says. "He means a lot to you."

"Yeah."

"It's mutual, you know." At my questioning look, she adds, "When he called to invite me to your party, he spoke very highly of you."

"He would," I say with a small smile.

"How did the two of you meet?"

Where to start? I'm stunned by how normal the conversation is. Maybe it's the hour and the dark. Maybe I'm just too worn out to feel the rage she stirs in me. I start at the beginning, from the day she left me at my grandmother's.

It takes hours. Hours in which George sleeps and she listens.

I have things to say. Things I've saved up for six years.

And I say them all.

Day five: My voice goes in the wee hours, sounding ugly and raw.

That's when she takes over.

"I love you, Sophie. If I could take it all back, and take you with me, I would. I made a mistake."

She tells me how her life was changed by that decision. Uncle Eddy reenlisted at some point. Despite everything, she became a soldier's wife again. Then the cancer hit. This is his third time in remission in six years. And she's been through it all alone because she lost every single friend she ever had when she walked out on our family.

I hear my father's voice again.

Sometimes a moment defines you, defines how people see you the rest of your life.

That day she left me at my grandmother's—that was my mother's moment, and she didn't realize it until it was too late.

She doesn't make excuses. That would be insulting, and I think she knows it.

As the sun peeks through the blinds and the hospital begins to wake, she finally says, "I need to tell you something. Something that will upset you, but I think you deserve to know the truth."

And that's when she tells me how she'd realized she'd made a mistake leaving with Uncle Eddy, and how she'd begged my father to see me in those early years. She reveals how he refused to let her see me, making sure I was never home when she came, and how he threatened to move me away from Sweethaven if she tried to see me without him. He told her I hated her. And she confesses that she let herself believe him because it was easier to think I hated her than to admit how she'd failed me.

She broke his heart, and my father hated her so much, he took me.

And that, I realize, was my father's defining moment.

I'm not sure what to say to my mother. She's stunned me,

and yet so much of it makes sense. I can't excuse her, but as she speaks, I remember times my father shuttled me off to my grandmother's or Carey's without notice. I thought he wanted to get rid of me, but the truth has more layers.

My mother leaves to refill George's plastic pitcher of water, and I watch her go with a more open mind. I'm so exhausted, I don't know what to feel. Outside, a crow flies past the window before disappearing into the trees.

George makes a noise, and I stand to check on him.

He's not asleep like I thought. His watery gray eyes are wide open and staring right into mine.

It's not at all like the movies—there's no dramatic music or doctors running in the room—but I know.

One crow, I think. *One for sorrow.*

"George," I say, squeezing his hand.

He doesn't respond. Nurse Espinoza enters the room and checks the myriad of machines they've hooked to his body. She warned me how this would go. George doesn't want to be resuscitated, and they won't take measures to save him. When our eyes meet, she nods. Without a word, she turns the volume off so we won't hear George dying, one blip at a time.

I turn my face away for a moment, digging for strength.

Then I pull myself up onto George's bed, and I lean my face next to his. I talk to him about nothing. I tell him I love him. I thank him. I promise to make him proud. I say how proud I am that he's my family.

A sound comes from deep within his body and rattles from his throat.

He gasps for air.

I kiss his cheek.

Good-bye, friend.

Chapter Thirty

The day after George dies, CNN reports Carey's condition as stable. He will return home.

Relief mixes with grief in one deep well. I cry.

My mother takes charge. She's a soldier's wife, despite all that's happened, and she keeps everything together when I fall apart. Like a well-heeled general, she moves me from one place to another with supreme efficiency. Not even my father gets in her way. He disappears into his study and doesn't come out, even when she temporarily moves into our house, sleeping on the couch and putting meals on the table when she can coax food into me.

I never see them exchange more than two polite words.

George has no family. Pierce Whitney, an old friend of his, introduces himself as a lawyer from Raleigh and the executor of George's will. George arranged his funeral long ago, planning it right down to the guest list (Nurse Espinoza is to wear a short dress and sit in the front row next to me) and the music he wanted played (none of that weepy, sentimental bullshit).

I don't give the eulogy.

I can't.

Instead, Private Don Baruth and a series of soldiers from every armed force march to the podium. Each has a favorite George story, a favorite George joke, a favorite moment that was so George. Nurse Espinoza holds my hand, and we share a smile as the music comes on.

And hearing it, I choke, causing heads to turn.

My entire body shakes as I hunch over, tipping my face into my hands. My mother's arm comes around me, and I can feel her leaning over in concern.

A few uncomfortable titters start up from the far corner as people begin to pay attention to the lyrics of the rap song playing through the church. I collapse in a fit of giggles, gasping for air, and I don't care when people stare.

Somewhere, somehow, George found a song to play just for me.

The rapper repeats, "Yo Mama" for the fourth time, and I'm crying and laughing at the same time.

Fuck, I'm going to miss you, George.

At the cemetery, seven soldiers fire three times each, giving George a twenty-one-gun salute. The honor guard removes the flag from George's casket, folding it in perfect creases until it forms a triangle.

Pierce says George asked for the flag to go to me, so when a member of the honor guard bends down to hand the folded flag to me, I take it.

The Marine's voice is clear and calm. "On behalf of the President of the United States and the people of a grateful nation, I present this flag as a token of appreciation for the honorable and faithful service your loved one rendered this nation."

A lone bugler plays taps.

Later, I find out that George left his estate to me, including all of his photos and equipment.

I do not feel worthy of either honor.

One night, about a week after the funeral, my mother decides it's time for her to go home. She can't leave Uncle Eddy alone any longer.

I'd returned to school days ago, and I only have a month or so before I graduate. Like a robot, I go through the motions, attending classes and doing homework and taking tests. What else is there to do? Blake ignores me for the most part when he actually comes to school, and I no longer have the desire to fix what's broken between us.

Then at dinner on my mom's last night, she says, "Come live with me."

I drop my fork, staring at her, wondering if she's kidding. She swirls her glass of wine, peering into the ruby liquid as if to divine my answer there.

"Mom—"

"You're going to college in the fall, so it would only be a few months. But I want the chance to know you again, Sophie."

I have no idea what to say. My thoughts barely look ahead to putting on my pajamas at the end of the day, let alone what I will be doing in a few months. Nothing is easy between us.

Her blue eyes plead. "Just think about it. That's all I'm asking. It might be a good thing to have a change of scenery."

She leaves, and for the first time in weeks, I am alone in the house with my father.

A short pause follows my knock on his study door before he calls, "Come in."

He hides behind his desk with a pile of folders laid out in front of him. Things have changed: I've changed. I'm no longer afraid of him hating me. After all, it was never *me* he saw when he looked at me. And I am more than a poor copy of her.

I set a covered plate of food on the desk. "Mom left this for you."

He shoots me a questioning look.

"She's gone," I say. "Back to Uncle Eddy."

We have tiptoed around this conversation for days. Maybe for years. Without a chair to sit in, I stand. Rather than retreating, I walk the perimeter of the room, trailing my fingers over the books on his Wall of War.

"What's on your mind, Quinn?" he asks, leaving the plate untouched.

He watches me warily, and I drop my hands to my sides. I won't fidget like I'm the guilty party. "She told me she tried to see me. That you wouldn't let her see me."

Such a strong Marine, my father. He does not betray his emotions the slightest. His voice remains calm and even. "And? You expect me to apologize for that?"

"No." I shake my head. That would be like holding my breath until the sun stopped shining. I don't even expect answers. "I just wanted to know if it was the truth."

"I knew this would happen. Your mom shows up, and you think she's some kind of hero. She'll disappoint you. That's why I kept her away."

"Then it is true."

A muscle works along his jaw when he clenches his teeth. "I did what I thought was best."

"Did you, Daddy?" I ask. I hug my arms about my body. "Because from where I stood, I thought you hated me." I start crying. "Do you know how much I've hated that I look like her? Do you think I didn't know what you've thought of me these last months? A slut just like Mom?"

My father stands, slapping both hands flat on the desk as he glares at me. "Sophie Topper Quinn, I won't hear you speak like that in my house."

He sounds angry, like when I was a child and he would draw out my name to let me know how much trouble I was in.

Sophie Topper Quinn, for a spanking and a week grounded.

Sophie Quinn, for no TV and early to bed.

And, once upon a time, I was just Sophie, for love and kisses and my arms around his neck after six months apart.

Quietly I say, "So you do remember my name? I wasn't sure anymore."

My father says nothing. I've pushed him too far. He will not engage. I leave him in his office, but before I go I tell him, "She's asked me to move in with her until I leave for college."

I wait. For anger. For blame. For a crack to show. But there is only rebar reinforcing steel. Big, strong Lieutenant Colonel Cole Quinn is too weak to talk about the past.

The movies have everything wrong, it turns out.

Those big reunions where everyone apologizes and the family lives happily ever after? They're such bullshit.

The truth is, some apologies never see the light of day.

On my way to my room, the phone rings. I pick up the receiver of our old rotary phone from the table in the hall. "Hello?"

"Quinn."

His voice sinks me to the floor like a stone to the bottom of a pond.

"Carey."

"It's Mr. Breen, Quinn."

The difference in their voices finally penetrates. No, not Carey at all.

"Hi, Mr. Breen. How is he?" Carey's parents have been

in Germany with him, sending bits of news back to the town through Blake. It's taken two weeks. Two weeks for one of them to call me.

There's a long pause. Finally, he says, "Well. As well as can be expected, considering."

That is not the same as "good" or "better," but I'll take it.

"I'm glad," I say. "I've been worried about him."

And it's true. Staying home after George died, there had been nothing to do except watch the news, raking through reports on Carey for some tidbit of truth. Everything's "he's a hero," but nobody will speak of how said hero is holding up. He would hate the kind of attention he's getting.

There's another pause. When Mr. Breen speaks, it's like the words are pulled out of him. "He asked me to call you."

Mr. Breen did not want to make this call, I realize. Did not want to speak to me.

My heart sinks. I wait, and Mr. Breen does not disappoint me.

"He asked me to give you a message."

"Did he?" I ask. It's so obvious Mr. Breen thinks he's passing along a message to his son's cheating ex, and it makes me physically sick. Carey's back, but he's still keeping secrets.

"He said to tell you he can't do what you asked. Maybe someday, but not now."

Anger sweeps through me, burning everything in its path, but it puffs out suddenly in a smoke-ridden cloud of grief. My best friend has let me down. He's let his family, my family, and all our friends think the worst of me. Perhaps it's expecting too much of him to admit the truth right now, after everything he's been through. And yet . . . it kills me that his father must think I've asked Carey to forgive my cheating ways. Condemnation rings in his voice, and I can't swallow any more shame.

Suddenly I am done. I have nothing left to give Carey. He's taken everything. All my self-respect and pride. Him, Blake, my parents. The only person who didn't steal a piece of me is dead.

"Mr. Breen," I say, "will you tell him something for me?"

His silence is angry, but he grunts in assent.

"Tell Carey . . . tell him I said not to bother."

"Excuse me?" he says, confused.

"I really hope he gets well, Mr. Breen. I can't imagine what he's been through these past months. I know he's a hero, and I'm so proud of him for that." I can't believe I'm saying my second good-bye in as many weeks. "But he's let me down. And I can't . . ." I break on a sob, one of those hiccuping ones that dissolves into a series of sighs.

"Quinn?" Mr. Breen asks, and finally there is an ounce of concern in his voice. Too little, too late.

I take a deep breath. "My name is Sophie."

With shaking fingers, I hang up the phone, covering my face as I cry.

Down the hall, my father closes the door to his study.

Chapter Thirty-One

It's June now, and I'm leaving Sweethaven.

There's nothing left for me here, and I feel like I will never be able to make a fresh start in this town. I will always be Sophie Topper Quinn, the slut who cheated on our hero. So between school and my work at the hospital, I pack my life into boxes and crates that will go to my mother's.

Sweethaven High has come alive, buzzing with news of Carey coming stateside. Mrs. Breen takes a leave of absence to move to Bethesda so she can be near him at the hospital in Maryland where he will make his recovery. I am happy for him. Happy he's pulling through and happy his mother will have her son back.

But I am not happy.

I'd always thought school would end with a bang. An explosion of trashed homework, fond memories, and signed yearbooks.

Instead, I've regained my magical powers of invisibility. With Carey found, I'm no longer important.

I am merely a blip in his primetime *20/20* story—the part before he became a hero.

On the last day of school, I clean out my locker, piling my few belongings into my bag. I've never left much in the locker, for fear that Jamie would destroy everything, so it doesn't take long. I snap the door shut one last time, and my hand lingers on the marks scratched into the surface. Mr. Dupree had done his best to paint over the words, but I can still make them out.

TRAITOR.

WHORE.

I wish the words didn't hurt. The best I can say is that I no longer believe they are true.

"Hey, Q."

Angel stands behind me when I turn. At some point in the past weeks, she's gone back to her brunette color. It looks better on her than the cool blond she's worn all year.

"Hey, Ang."

"I bet you're glad to get out of here," she says, nodding at my locker.

I shrug.

"I heard you're moving to live with your mom."

So they are still talking about me. The only people I've told are my parents. But then, I've had to buy boxes and supplies to pack my things. And I guess I should have expected gossip to fly with my mother popping up around town. She's determined to be part of my life, and she doesn't care who knows it.

"Yeah," I say.

"Well . . ."

Angel's reaching for something to say. Maybe she wants me to excuse how she treated me, or how she let the others treat me. Then again, I've seen her with Blake lately and maybe the two of them are together now and she suspects something about us. She could just want to bridge the gaping hole in our friendship. Whatever she wants, I'm not the person to give it to her anymore.

I'm moving on.

I zip up my bag, toss it over my shoulder, and give my locker one last, hard look.

"Q?" she asks, when I walk away.

"Good-bye, Ang," I say. "Take care of yourself."

And I leave her and this whole miserable place behind.

Graduation moves me more than I thought it would.

Not because getting my diploma feels like being handed the key to the cell I've been locked in; it's only a little of that. Mostly I'm freaked out by my father, mother, and Uncle Eddy sitting out with the families in the crowd. They do not sit near each other—that would cause hell to freeze over—but they're in the same town and the same gymnasium.

That's enough. That's a lot.

After the ceremony, my father takes me out to dinner. It's my choice because I felt I owed him that much, and it's my last night in our house together. Since I told him I was moving, he's been quiet. Too quiet. They haven't been the punishing silences of the last year, but more thoughtful silences. I catch him watching me with an emotion I can't read.

Dinner is strange, with lots of awkward pauses. When we get home, my father enters the house ahead of me, and I wander out to his garden shed, glad for the reprieve. With everything that's happened, I've never switched the bottles of plant food and weed killer back. He's remained mystified by the barren state of his garden.

I should feel guilty, and I do, a little. Enough that I toss the two containers in the trash, feeling a pang of regret for taking the one thing he loves from him.

But I wanted so much from my father, and he disappointed me.

Some people just don't have it to give, though.

I sit on the porch to catch my breath in the evening summer heat, curling up on the swing where Carey once turned my life upside down. Tucking my skirt around my legs, I'm half-asleep when I hear a truck pull up.

Blake doesn't get out right away. He stares at me through the windshield, and I think maybe he's been crying. Even from this distance, I can see how red his eyes are. He finally gets out and I meet him on the steps, clenching my hand around the banister for support.

"Is Carey okay?" I ask, worried.

His hands clench into fists.

"Blake?"

"Yeah." He laughs, but the sound of it is angry. "That bastard is just fine. I just got off the phone with him. He told me the truth, Q."

Shocked, I sit on the top step with a thump that jars me. "What are you talking about?"

"He's gay. He's fucking gay, and he let you take the rap for him this year. He says he didn't know how everyone treated you, that you never told him. But fuck, what did he expect?"

"You told him?" I ask, though I can see the answer on his face.

"Every damned insult," he says vehemently. "The ones I know about anyway."

Well, I think. *At last.* I should feel vindicated. Triumphant because the truth is out. I can't figure out what emotions are winding through me, but none of them resemble happiness. I wonder who else knows and what the consequences will be for Carey.

"I want to hate him," Blake continues, sitting on a step below mine. "But he cried like I was breaking his damned heart. I've never heard him cry."

He shakes his head. "How could he lie to me like that, Q?"

"Sophie," I say quietly.

"What?" he says.

"My name is Sophie. Not Quinn. Not Q. It's Sophie."

Nobody gets why this is important to me, but I'm done

being who they think I should be. I am Sophie, whether they like it or not.

"Okay," he says, sounding confused.

"I don't think he lied," I answer. "Not to hurt you, anyway. Maybe he hid who he was because he didn't know if you'd still be his friend."

Blake glares. "That's bullshit. Like I care about that crap."

"Hey," I say, holding up my hands. "I didn't say that's what I thought. I said maybe that's what Carey thought. Imagine how I felt when he told me."

His shoulders stiffen, and I say, "You're angry at me."

"I guess I don't understand why you'd cover for him. Why do you always put him first?" Blake asks. He's not accusing, but sadness thickens his voice.

"You tell me. You did the same thing," I remind him gently. He looks down, and I hug myself. "It's a bad habit I'm trying to break. I suggest you do the same."

I explain about the night Carey came to me, beaten and bloody. He sacrificed so much to serve, and what did it get him? Even knowing that, my guess is that he'd do it again because, like George, Carey believed in something bigger than himself.

"I didn't know what else to do, Blake. Do you know how hard it was to see Carey like that? What would you have done in my place?"

After a while he says, "He told me about the night he confessed the truth. The night you and I . . ."

His voice trails off, and I sigh. "I'm sorry. I'm not proud of my reasons for going to you that night."

He swallows. I know I've hurt him when he asks, "Did you ever feel anything for me?"

I kneel down in front of him, placing my hands on his knees. I wait for him to meet my eyes. "That first night, I was confused. I didn't know what the hell I felt, except a lot of pain. But I figured things out pretty quick." I touch his cheek, stroking my fingers across his whiskered skin. "I fell in love with you, Blake."

He twines his fingers through mine, his eyes serious. "You never said. Even after that night in Grave Woods."

That surprises me. I thought I'd told him how I felt. "Is that why you've been ignoring me?" I ask.

"Yes. I couldn't wait around for you to toss me aside again. Especially once we heard Carey was coming home."

"I'm sorry. I never meant to hurt you."

"Ditto," he says.

He tugs me into his arms. Maybe we are both thinking about the damage the three of us have done to one another. Best friends, lost friends. When I can't take the tension anymore, I move to sit beside him. Blake's shoulder brushes mine, and sparks zing through me. I wonder if that will ever go away and know I will miss it if it does.

Suddenly his tone is fierce. "Do you think we could start over?"

Part of me wants to. Desperately wants to. I would love to give us a chance to put aside everything that's happened and see where we could end up. But another part of me knows that the wounds we've inflicted are too deep. We can't pretend they don't exist.

And I need to leave. If I stay in Sweethaven to be with him, I will be putting him first. Substituting Blake for Carey. I can't do it. I need to be first for once.

He can read my answer on my face and sighs. "I had to ask. I should go."

He stands, and I notice his T-shirt for the first time. In cursive writing, it reads *Third grade lied, I never use cursive.* I smile and shake my head, climbing to my feet on the step above him. I really do love him.

"Blake?"

He turns to face me, and I kiss him, surprising him. With sudden strength he pulls me closer, squeezing the breath out of me. And then he holds me for a long time with my head on his shoulder. Another good-bye.

My heart breaks a little more.

Finally he steps back and walks to his truck, opening the door. I call out, "Why did he tell you now? Carey, I mean. Why confess he's gay now?"

Blake shrugs. "I don't know. Something about a message you gave his father. He said he'd let you down by asking you to cover for him. And me."

Before he climbs into his truck, he gives me one last, long look. "I'm going to miss you, you know?"

"No, you won't," I say lightly. "You'll forget all about me."

He shakes his head. "Never. I love you, Sophie."

He says it like a promise, and closes his door before I can respond. I watch his truck disappear around the corner, and when he's gone I rise, brushing off my skirt.

I find my father standing in the open doorway. I think he's overheard enough to guess the truth when his shoulders drop. He knows what I did for Carey. He knows I'm not who he thought I was. And I didn't have to break my promise to tell him.

I wait for him to say something, and when he does, I'm stunned.

"I'm sorry," my father says, his voice cracking. "I was wrong."

And the world turns upside down and everything I think I know about people flips end to end once more.

Sometimes people *can* admit when they're wrong.

I hear George's voice. *You're the one in control here. Be kind.*

I walk into my father's arms, and he says, "Please forgive me, Sophie."

Chapter Thirty-Two

Since Carey came out to his family and friends two months ago, everything has changed.

My "friends" crawled out of the woodwork, calling me to commiserate about what I went through. Few of them apologized for their part in it, including Nikki, who reprimanded me for not telling her the truth. I hung up on her.

Angel, on the other hand, wouldn't stop apologizing. Pragmatically I asked, "How could you have known what I couldn't tell you?"

My own response came as the biggest surprise. Released from lying, I do not feel the urge to scream the truth from the mountaintops. The people I care about are the ones who believed in me all along—like George. The rest of them no longer matter. And I've come to realize something: George was right; I was the one in control all along. I kept Carey's secret, but nobody really forced me to do it.

As for Carey . . . he hasn't called. At first, the media swarmed around him. The MIA Marine found alive after months of torture. For weeks, daily reports shared how he was recovering, until one day it seemed like the world outside of Sweethaven forgot he existed.

Then, about a week before I'm to move to Boston, Mrs. Breen calls. Before I can say more than hello, she launches into a breathless plea.

Carey isn't recovering at all. He's refusing to do his physical therapy, and the doctors say he won't walk if he continues on that way. Days, he sits in his room, staring at the walls. Nights, he wakes screaming from nightmares about things he won't speak of. He's dying in front of her, and she doesn't know what to do, God help her.

She's sorry, she says. Carey needs me, but he won't let anyone call me. She will get down on her knees and beg if it will help. *Please, please,* she says, and she sobs.

And I tell her I'm on my way.

It takes more than six hours to drive from North Carolina to Bethesda, Maryland.

My mother didn't want me to make the drive alone. She fussed over me, pointing out every car accident or carjacking that had been in the news in the past five years, until my father finally told her, "Sophie, let the girl alone. If anyone can take care of herself, she can."

They do not get along well, but they try for my sake. My father still won't talk to Uncle Eddy, and I can't say I blame him. I don't talk to Uncle Eddy much, either, despite living in his house. But if I've learned one thing this last year, it's that anything's possible.

George has made the unimaginable a reality for me. His lawyer had all of his photos and equipment delivered to my mother's over the summer. Upon opening the boxes, I discovered thousands upon thousands of negatives and prints. The majority were of wars in different countries, covering several decades. Most were of soldiers in varying states of weariness, heartbreak, joy, and despair.

I've decided to gather them into a book. I'm not sure if anyone will be interested in publishing it, but I feel like George has left me with this enormous responsibility to tell the stories of the sacrifices our service men and women make for our country. My father has agreed to help me, and we are working on it together. With his knowledge of military history, he's able to help me piece the images together in some kind of order.

Sometimes I see my father's hand linger over a particular picture, and I think of how George fell into memories the same way. I wonder, then, how much my father hides. If he experienced even a fraction of what George did, it's devastating.

Maybe someday I will interview him for the Veterans History Project.

When I arrive at the hospital to see Carey, I call my parents to let them know I'm there. Then I call Mrs. Breen.

"Thanks for coming, Sophie," she says. She meets me in the hospital lobby. She doesn't look any better than the last time I saw her crying in the hardware store aisle. Black bags droop under her eyes, and she's lost weight, considering how her clothes hang on her tiny frame.

"I'm not sure I'll be of any help," I warn. "You shouldn't expect much."

She shrugs. "Then we'll be no worse off than before."

We stand awkwardly waiting for the elevator. I used to love this woman, but now we can hardly look at each other.

"You seem different," she says finally as we're walking down the hall.

"I am different," I say, and it's true. I'm not the Quinn she used to know. That girl died, and Sophie was born out of her ashes.

We reach Carey's room, and I stop outside the doorway. After driving all this way, suddenly I'm scared. I'm not sure this is the right thing to do. I back away, losing my nerve. More than scared, I'm ashamed, I realize. I kept Carey's secret, but he's given so much more than me. He chose to risk his life for his country, even though he had to hide a huge part of himself.

"Sophie?" she asks, concerned.

"He hasn't wanted to see me before. What makes you think he'll want to now?"

Mrs. Breen gives me a piercing look. "He's been asking for you since they found him."

I stare at her in shock.

She sighs. "When I first saw that picture of you, I couldn't believe you would do that to Carey. The way the two of you were together—I thought you would always be that way. As his mother, I was selfishly glad that you would always be there for him. I hated you for hurting him. So I lied to him. I told him you didn't want to see him."

I open my mouth and close it three times when the only things I can think to say are all curses. As angry as I'd been with Carey, I would never have refused to see him.

Mrs. Breen stops me. "I know I made a mistake. I thought he would get past it, but once he told us what you did for him, I . . ."

She folds her hands, twisting her fingers until they form a white knuckled knot. This is where a bigger person might forgive her. Maybe go so far as to comfort her. I am not that person. I pull away from her touch. I want to throw up. What must Carey have thought when she told him that lie?

"Go away," I tell her.

"Sophie . . . ," she says.

"Don't worry," I say coldly. "I'm going to see him. But not for you."

She backs away from me, and I watch her until she disappears around a corner. I feel mean. I feel angry enough to rip into her. This isn't how I want Carey to see me, and so I take deep breaths to calm myself.

I square my shoulders and walk into his room.

He doesn't notice me right away, and I barely hold in my gasp at the changes in him.

Carey always had a laugh waiting on his lips. Now his eyes droop with sadness as he stares unseeing out the window. His mouth pulls down at the corners, and he lies stiff and silent in his bed, with one leg wrapped in a white brace. Below his shorts, there are scars striping both legs, and I wonder what his torturers did to him. The bruises they showed on the news have faded, but everything about him screams BROKEN.

George said you can't understand what a soldier experiences unless you've been through it yourself. The closest you can come is to hear their stories. That's why it was so important for him to tell them. To help people understand, so maybe they will treat soldiers differently. So people will show soldiers a little mercy and grace when they come home, not as they were, but as strangers taking the place of your loved ones.

Mercy and grace, I think. And maybe it's time I ask for a little forgiveness, because I've taken for granted all that he was willing to give up. Once more, I'm glad that I knew George because, without him, I would not know what to do at this moment.

I step forward.

"Carey?"

He rolls his head to face me, and his brown eyes look dead. Until they focus on me.

"Quinn?" he asks, disbelieving.

I don't correct him. I don't need to tell Carey who I am. He knows.

"It's me," I say. I drop my purse on the floor and stop by the side of his bed. His hand is cold in mine, and I twine my fingers through his. "I missed you."

He reaches for me, clamping a hand around my neck to pull me to him, until my forehead rests against his. The desperation in his eyes makes my own water.

"Where have you been?" he asks.

"I thought you didn't want to see me," I say.

"I thought you hated me."

I swallow. "No. I'm sorry about that message I gave your father." I force a smile. "I love you, stupid."

Whatever has kept him glued together these past months comes unstuck. Carey falls to pieces in front of me. His shoulders heave, and he buries his face in my neck, grasping my shirt in his fists. He cries like he'll never stop. This isn't all about me. It's like seeing me has released something he's been holding in.

I don't know how to help him.

When I think about calling a nurse, he begs, "Don't go!"

And I realize this is another one of my defining moments.

So I kick off my shoes and crawl up next to Carey on the

bed. I hold his hand. I tell him how much I love him. I tell him how proud I am of him. I apologize for not being a better friend. I tell him how I've always known that we would be friends until we were eighty and rocking away in our chairs on a porch somewhere.

Later, when he's calm, I ask him about Afghanistan.

We talk all night, two friends getting to know each other again.

And it's a beginning.

Author's Note

If you were inspired by Quinn's experience, please consider interviewing a veteran in your life and community. The Veterans History Project (VHP) at www.loc.gov/vets provides straightforward guidelines and the required forms you'll need to complete an interview and ensure it is submitted to the Library of Congress, where it will be preserved and shared for posterity. On the website you'll also find a Field Kit Companion Video that explains the VHP process, offers tips to make the VHP experience meaningful for both the volunteer and the veteran, and elaborates on what happens to collections after they reach the Library of Congress.

To get involved with the US Department of Veterans Affairs facility nearest you and to learn how you might work with someone like George, www.volunteer.va.gov/ is a great place to start.

Acknowledgments

I have so many people to thank.

This book wouldn't be what it is without the support of my Spalding MFA mentor, Mary Yukari Waters. Your insights pushed me, and your letters made me laugh, especially the one where you wrote "THIS IS CRAP" across the top.

Thank you to my agent, Laura Bradford, who didn't freak out when it took me a year to write this book. You meant it when you said you stick by your writers, and I am ever so grateful.

Dear Annette Pollert, my wonderful, brilliant editor, how do you thank someone for making your dreams come true? If you'll accept compensation in superawesome highlighters, you'll have my down payment shortly. Please share them with all the other great people at Simon Pulse who made this book happen, including Bethany Buck, Mara Anastas, Jennifer Klonsky, Lucille Rettino, Carolyn Swerdloff, Dawn Ryan, Paul Crichton,

Anna McKean, Katherine Devendorf, Brenna Franzitta, Angela Goddard, Mary Marotta, Christina Pecorale, Maria Faria, Brian Kelleher, Jim Conlin, Teresa Brumm, and Victor Iannone.

To my first readers—Stephanie Kuehn, Laurie Devore, Debra Driza, Jay Lehmann, Dawn Rae Miller, Roger Perez, Veronica Roth and the Write Nighters—your critiques made me cry in a GOOD way. I reread my favorite comments in moments of crisis. I also owe Erica Henry and Abby Stevens gratitude for aiding me with my military research.

I can't say enough about Spalding University's MFA program. You offer a nurturing place in which to be creative and grow. In particular, I want to thank those who workshopped the first chapters of this book, including Julie Brickman, Omar Figueras, Michael Morris, Teddy Jones, and Krista Humphrey.

To my day job companions, especially Michelle Yovanovich, Lori Leiva, Tony Tomassini, and Scott Sawicki—thank you for supporting me on my journey. You didn't even mind when I got a book deal and shrieked the office down.

My dear bro-in-law, Stephen Curto, you've encouraged me since I wrote my first short story in the third grade, and you told me not to give up. Fotang, man.

My gratitude also goes to the Veterans History Project, including Jeffrey Lofton and Monica Mohindra, for the great work they do preserving the stories of our soldiers.

Huge heartfelt thanks to the Marines who took the time to answer my many questions, though you asked to remain nameless.

Your courage awes me. Stay safe and be well. This book was also inspired in part by my late uncle, PFC Daniel Vaché, and my honorary uncle, SPC John Curtis. Your sacrifices in Vietnam aren't forgotten.

Last, but never least, thanks to my family for believing in me. Not one of you acted surprised when I called to tell you about my book deal, and that meant everything. Mom, Kymberli, Michael, Kenny, Aunt Susie, Stephen, and all the nieces and nephews, I love you more than books.

About the Author

CORRINE JACKSON lives in San Francisco, where she works at a top marketing agency managing marketing campaigns for several Fortune 500 clients. She has bachelor's and master's degrees in English, and an MFA in Creative Writing from Spalding University. *If I Lie* is her debut novel. Visit her at corrinejackson.com or on Twitter at @Cory_Jackson.